SHOCK WAVE

KEITH TAYLOR

CHAPTER ONE

FAREWELL, FRISCO

YOU'RE LOOKING DOWN into a pool of gray, murky water.

At its widest point the pool... Scratch that. *Pool* conjures up far too pleasant an image. It doesn't belong here, where the air smells stale and the dim, washed-out light seems second-hand. This is a *swamp*. It's a bleak, foul, waterlogged ditch the color of old dishwater, and at its widest point it reaches dozens of yards across before the milky liquid begins to seep into the mud at its fringes.

You can see dim moonlight against the water's surface, but the reflection isn't clear. It's rippled and disturbed by a gray chemical scum, an odious, stinking spume that clings to the surface and releases the stench of waste with every silently bursting bubble. Somewhere nearby you hear the sound of a broken sewer main emptying its effluent into the water.

You pull back, and now you see that the ditch is far below ground level. You're in a hole, a dark crater burrowed thirty yards deep into the earth, its shallow sides a mess of wet mud, shattered concrete and twisted steel.

You rise up, relieved to leave the airless swamp behind, and you see that beyond the lip of the crater the ground has been scoured clear. Every building, road and blade of grass – everything that suggests there was once life – has been razed. All that remains is dust and death.

In the dim moonlight you can see only a shadow of what once stood here. The foundations of buildings reduced to rubble. The ordered grid of city streets stripped of their asphalt. The burned, empty carcasses of cars, trams and trucks. Their remains exist only as a memorial.

Now the air is thick with the billow of greasy smoke, choking and blinding. You recoil from the acrid, toxic bite in the back of your throat, and you rise higher to escape the dust that fills your lungs and burns your skin. A pall of it still clings close to the ground, floating like a mist, kicked up in the stale breeze and refusing to settle.

You're higher now, far above the ground, and here you gain a new perspective on the ravaged landscape stretching out around you. Now you see that the crater is at the center of it all. The scoured earth spreads out from there in all directions, a ragged circle a mile across, and it's only at the edge of this barren patch that you begin to see buildings still standing, walls crumbling and windows blown out. There are fires raging out there, almost exhausted but still searching hungrily for fuel.

Now you begin to recognize the city.

This used to be San Francisco.

To the west the green has been scorched away, but you can still make out the long, narrow rectangle of Golden Gate Park. Now it's just an empty patch that stretches halfway across the city, ending abruptly at the debris-strewn beach. To the north you see Presidio, and beyond it the iconic majesty of the Golden Gate Bridge, scoured of its color and shrouded in a thick layer of ash, but somehow still standing.

It's now that you begin to notice the people. Bodies, mostly. Some of them are half buried in rubble, others simply collapsed on the ground, dying where they fell, but all of them are shrouded in the same gray, choking ash that even now falls from the sky. The smell of burned rubber and scorched brick dust is difficult to bear, but at least it hides the gag inducing odor of burned flesh.

In amongst the corpses there are some people still moving. Just a few, most of them far from the crater where the buildings were better shielded. Through broken windows and collapsed walls you catch the occasional glimpse of flames and flashlights picked out against the darkness. The people huddle around their fires, stoking them with an almost religious fervor, as if they'll somehow be safe just as long as they can keep the darkness at bay.

If you move closer you might hear the weeping, the moans and screams of pain, the frantic, whispered prayers, but you're not curious. You don't want to hear the hope in their voices, because you know there *is* no hope for them. It would have been much kinder if they'd been taken quickly. Now they're cursed to suffer before the end comes, and this end will be much slower and much, *much* more painful than the instant mercy of a nuclear blast. Soon enough these prayers for life will become desperate, pleading prayers for death.

You turn away from them now, further from the crater and the burned out buildings, out towards the crumbling high rises to the east. There are more people here, some of them still on their feet, emerging from the basements and underground parking lots that protected them from the blast. Most of them are searching for lost loved ones or planning their escape, and their hope is even stronger. These people believe they might yet survive, but they'll learn the truth soon enough. The poisoned ruins have already sealed their fate.

As you move further east you pause for a moment, curious at the sight of a cluster of bodies around the charred remains of Union Square. Most of the dead in the city seem to have fallen alone, but this is the first group you've seen. Hundreds of them huddle close to each other in gutted stores, their bodies seemingly posed like mannequins in macabre window displays. There's still movement here, but when you look closer you see it's mostly rats. They were wise enough to seek shelter when the air turned to fire.

Now you rise up and begin to leave the burned

carcass of the city behind. There's nothing but death back there. Across the water you see Oakland, Berkeley and Alameda, and on the far side of the bay it looks like life goes on. The streetlights still shine, and the buildings still stand.

There are few people out there, though. Those who could leave fled long ago, but here and there a vehicle moves silently between inviting pools of light. You move towards them, eager to leave behind the stench of death and ensconce yourself in the comforting warmth of–

Wait.

Something catches your eye.

Far below you see that the western half of the Bay Bridge has collapsed into the black water. The entire structure has vanished beneath the roiling waves, and all that's left is a lip of shattered concrete reaching out just a few yards from the Yerba Buena tunnel. At the mouth of the tunnel you see something cut through the layer of ash that blankets the crumbling edge.

Fresh footprints. Three pairs, two large and one small.

Somebody actually *survived*. Against incredible odds three people somehow escaped the collapse of the bridge, lived through the blast and survived long enough to leave footprints in the fresh fallout that blankets the ground like virgin snow. You move in closer, your curiosity piqued, and as you approach the gaping tunnel mouth you see that the prints vanish into the darkness within.

A dim glow catches your eye deep within the tunnel. Curiosity pulls you forward, and as you move toward it you notice the outline of a steel door in the tunnel wall, framed by the green glow of an emergency exit sign. Beyond the door a staircase leads down, carved into the rock, its walls glowing blood red under emergency lights. You move down, deeper underground, and now you hear something you weren't expecting.

You hear somebody breathing. Panting. You hear the rustle of heavy clothing and the sound of boots on stone.

You round a corner, and now you see her.

It's a woman, almost buried in a bright yellow work jacket made for someone a foot taller and a hundred pounds heavier. She struggles up the red-lit staircase in boots three sizes too big, her long blond hair tucked beneath a hard hat, the collar of her jacket turned up to cover her neck.

You move closer, and now you see she's injured,

exhausted, fighting through the pain as she forces her bruised body up the staircase. Closer still, and you see pallid skin. She looks so weak she could collapse at any moment.

Even closer now, so close that you could reach out and touch her, and finally you see the determination in her red-rimmed eyes. You don't know who she is, but you can see that some powerful force is driving her, something beyond sight that keeps her putting one foot in front of the other despite the pain. Some reason to fight for survival that goes beyond self preservation.

You can see in her eyes that she's a mother.

•▼•

CHAPTER TWO

THE FLOOR IS LAVA

KAREN STARED UP at the final dozen steps, her eyes fixed firmly on the door at the top with the determination of a climber setting her sights on a mountain peak. She gripped the handrail in both hands like a taut rope, hauling herself up the dimly lit shaft on trembling legs.

Her body was screaming out for rest. Her bruised ribs stabbed at her chest with each quick, shallow breath, but still she forced herself to climb onward. There was no time to spare. She couldn't allow herself the luxury of catching her breath while her daughter breathed poisoned air in the control room far below.

The last few steps seemed to stretch out above her

for an eternity. In her mind they grew to the height of towering cliffs, looming over her, impossible to scale, but somehow she summoned the strength to drag herself to the top. When her hands finally touched the cold steel of the door she let out a relieved laugh, echoing eerily down the stairwell, then quickly silenced herself as she raised her radio to her lips.

"Doc," she whispered, fearful of her voice carrying to the other side, "do you see anybody out there?"

She gnawed nervously on a nail as she waited for his reply, then pulled her hand from her mouth with a look of disgust when she realized what she was doing. Her nails were gray, packed with the ground in dirt she hadn't been able to wash away in the bathroom. There was no way of knowing if it was radioactive.

"*Doc*," she whispered again, harshly, picking at the dirt with a thumbnail. "Are you reading me?"

When the reply finally came through Ramos' voice crackled with interference, the signal struggling to make it through the yards of solid rock that separated her from the control room.

"Hang on a sec," he replied. "I can barely hear you. I'm panning the camera around."

For a long moment Karen stood staring at the door in front of her, worrying about what she'd find on the other side. In her imagination there were all kinds of threats waiting for her out there, from raging fires to deadly fallout, but the worst danger she could imagine was to find hundreds of people – sick, panicked and dangerous – eager to flood down the staircase to join Emily in their shelter. Whatever happened she couldn't let anyone put her daughter at risk.

Eventually Ramos came back, his voice faint and hard to make out.

"I can't see any movement from here. No promises, but it looks to me like you have a clear run all the way to the fans."

Karen sighed with relief. She didn't want any complications. On the other side of that door she knew she'd be fully exposed to the radiation raining down from the sky above the city. She knew she'd have to be quick if she wanted to make it back to Emily alive, and the last thing she needed was to stop for a chat with anyone unfortunate enough to still be out there. She didn't want to have to look them in the eye, knowing they'd already been handed a death sentence.

She took a deep breath and tugged her high visibility jacket tight around her waist.

"I'm going in," she whispered into the radio, leaning a shoulder against the heavy steel door. "Warn me if you see anyone on the cameras."

As the door swung open the acrid stink of exhaust fumes hit her right away, catching in the back of her throat and sending her staggering back into the stairwell. It was so thick it was almost a solid wall down at the bottom of the lower deck, and it was easy to see why. There were hundreds of cars within sight. As far as Karen could see they were all abandoned, but the drivers hadn't thought to kill their engines before they'd fled, and now the cars sat pumping out fumes that overwhelmed the ventilation fans. The smoke coiled and gathered like an eerie fog beneath the dim emergency lights glowing from the ceiling.

Karen tugged her collar over her mouth, trying to block out the smell and keep as much of her skin as she could protected from the ash she could see drifting in the air along with the exhaust, but she knew it was a futile gesture. There was no escaping the fumes, and Ramos had already explained over the radio as she climbed that it wasn't the ash she had to worry about. That was just the most visible danger, formed from the heaviest elements and first to fall from the sky.

By now the air *itself* was radioactive. Now that the ground had been completely blanketed by fallout it would have been picked up by the wind and scattered into particles far too small to see. It would have reached every inch of the tunnel, channeled through by natural air currents and the enormous fans designed to suck in air from the west and push it out the east.

By now the concrete walls of the tunnel, the steel door beside her and even the abandoned vehicles ahead would be buzzing with radiation, all of them shrouded in a fine coating of radioactive dust. She was entering a death zone. Nothing short of a radiation suit would keep her safe out here.

She stepped nervously out into the tunnel, hopping down to the road from the elevated lip of the door, and right away she could see motes of dust and wisps of smoke dancing in headlights. There was no way of knowing whether it was relatively harmless exhaust or deadly fallout, but it didn't matter. There was no escaping it. With every breath she'd be inhaling radioactive particles, and with every second she spent out here in the open she'd be taking one step closer to an excruciating death.

She pushed the door closed behind her, sealing off the staircase from the poisoned air now filling her lungs, and with a determined expression she turned east in the direction of Oakland.

"Doc, do you see me on screen?" Karen's voice came out strained and quiet as she tried to limit her breathing.

"Yeah, I see you," came the broken reply. "You're on camera 21."

"OK, which way should I walk?" She knew the ventilation fans were close to camera 23, but she had no idea which direction they were in, and she knew she didn't have the time to wander aimlessly through the tunnel until she found them.

The radio crackled again, the signal even weaker now she was on the wrong side of the door. "Can you give me a wave? High as you can reach. I'll look for you on 20 and 22."

Karen jumped and raised an arm towards the ceiling, the other clinging to the radio and the collar of her jacket. "Can you see me now, Doc?"

"No, all I can see is cars from here," Ramos replied, his voice almost silent now. "Can you get to higher ground? Maybe climb up on one of the cars?"

Karen cursed under her breath. She couldn't afford this delay. She could already feel the dust and grime settling on her skin, and in her head she could almost hear the frantic clicking of a Geiger counter warning of the radiation tearing through her body, ripping her DNA to shreds.

She turned to an old Cadillac sedan beside her, its engine still running, the exhaust belching out choking blue smoke, and as she tugged her sleeves over her bare hands and hoisted herself up onto the trunk a vivid memory came to her. She remembered playing as a child, hopping from her mom's couch to the armchair imagining that the floor was a creeping river of lava. She remembered the fake terror, squealing with mock pain as she stumbled from an armrest and touched the carpet.

This time it was real. This time, she thought with a fearful shiver, *everything* she touched would burn her.

She pulled herself to her feet on the trunk of the car, carefully brushing the ash from her knees before raising her arms high, waving above her head. After a long, tense silence the radio crackled.

"OK, I've got you," said Ramos. "I see you facing

away from me on camera 22. You need to turn around and head maybe a hundred yards west. The junction box is on the south wall. Got it?"

"Got it. Thanks, Doc." She dropped the radio back into the breast pocket of the jacket and hopped back down to the road. She barely had the energy to walk, but from somewhere deep down she dredged the strength to force herself into a clumsy jog in the narrow path between the cars. A hundred yards there and a hundred back, with maybe a couple of minutes to shut off the power to the fans.

That *might* be survivable, so long as she moved quickly.

The doc had explained the risks to her over the radio as she'd climbed the stairs. Within a half hour of the blast the worst of the fallout would already have returned to earth this close to ground zero, and they'd only been exposed to it for a couple of minutes before they'd reached shelter. Now the secret to survival was simply to stay sealed off from the outside world until the radiation decayed to relatively safe levels, and the way the Doc had described it made it sound as if it would be fairly easy, so long as they were smart about it.

Fallout, he said, decays incredibly fast. In the first

seven hours after the blast it would give up a massive 90% of its radiation. Seven times longer, by the forty ninth hour, and it would have expended 90% of what it had left, and by the three hundred thirty fourth hour – seven times longer than *that* – another 90% would have been spent. The upshot was that just a couple days after a nuclear blast the fallout would only be one hundredth as radioactive as it had been when it first touched the ground. A couple of weeks later and it would only have a thousandth of its original destructive power.

Surviving the horrors of nuclear fallout, Ramos said, was as simple as finding somewhere as isolated from the outside as possible and waiting it out for as long as your supplies lasted. The longer the better, but when it came down to it the worst of the danger would have passed by the end of a good game of Monopoly.

At first Karen hadn't believed Ramos when he said this. She'd been raised on dire warnings of the Cold War suddenly turning hot, on news reports of the Chernobyl meltdown and the sterile, irradiated ruins of Pripyat. She'd always believed that cities hit by nuclear disasters and attacks would crackle with radiation for generations, sealed off and avoided, but

Ramos assured her that the reality was nothing like that. After all, even Hiroshima had been rebuilt after the war, and today it was home to over a million people.

None of that helped Karen now, though, as she pushed herself to run faster between the rows of abandoned cars. She knew Ramos had only been trying to comfort her with meaningless information and half truths.

The only thing that really mattered was that right now the fallout was still at its most deadly, enough to kill with just minutes of exposure. Ramos had done his best to distract her with scientific jargon rather than tell her flat out whether or not she'd make it back alive, but when she'd demanded he give it to her straight he'd only said "If you can keep your exposure to below two hundred Roentgens you should be OK."

Karen had no idea what a Roentgen was, but from the nervous, brittle edge to Ramos' voice she guessed that she didn't *want* to know.

Up ahead she finally caught sight of the spinning fans in the roof of the tunnel, and beside them the thick black power cable running down the wall to the junction box. It had been three minutes since she'd stepped through the door. Another two to shut off the power, then one more to run back to safety. She could be home and dry in six minutes total.

Would it be enough?

As she neared the junction box Karen pulled her fire ax from a deep inner pocket of her jacket, scanning the steel case for the best place to break open the door, but when she drew beside it and reached out for the handle she was surprised to find that it wasn't locked. *So much for security*, she thought, swinging the door open to reveal a confusing mass of thick cables that vanished into the wall behind it.

But no switches. She'd expected to find something obvious, maybe a circuit breaker that could be tripped to cut off the power, or just a big red button that would shut everything down with a satisfying slap, but there was nothing like that. There was only the spaghetti mess of cables, all of them vanishing into the wall behind the junction box.

She reached out and tugged hard on an inch thick cable, hoping it might break away from the box, but all that happened was the insulated sheath slid a little over the wires beneath. She pulled harder, but she could already tell it wouldn't give. This, she realized with a sinking feeling, wasn't really a junction box. It was just a case designed to tidy the cables where they fed into the wall.

She raised the radio. "Doc," she whispered, fear gripping tight at her throat, "I think we have a problem here. I can't see any way to shut off the power."

A long moment of silence passed, broken only by hissing static from the radio, but no response came.

"Doc? Doc, do you hear me? I need your help!"

More silence. Now the panic really began to take hold. Karen felt her heart pound in her chest as she stared at the cables hanging from the wall. Above her she could hear the unrelenting spin of the fans, and she knew that with every lazy rotation they were pushing another dose of deadly fallout to her daughter below.

Whoomph.

There was another one. Another breath.

Whoomph.

Another step closer to death.

"Doc!" She was almost yelling now, her voice trembling as fear and frustration brought tears to her eyes, but still the only response was a maddening static hiss.

She shoved the radio back into her pocket, frustrated, and after a deep, calming breath she finally knew what she had to do. Even if Ramos could get through to her she knew there was nothing he could do to help. It was up to *her* to deal with this, and every moment those fans turned was another moment their shelter became less safe. Another moment Emily would be exposed to the radiation that would eventually kill her.

Karen felt the weight of the ax in her hands. It was small, more a hatchet than a true ax, but it felt like there was enough weight in its head to deliver a solid blow. She looked down at the steel handle, at the thick rubberized grip that covered it. Maybe it would be enough to protect her from the shock, or maybe it wouldn't, but there was only one way to find out. She couldn't afford to wait any longer.

She whispered a prayer as she drew the ax over her shoulder like a baseball bat, carefully sighting the thickest cable running from the fans into the back of the box, and as she swung her arms she gritted her teeth and let out a yelp.

The blade severed the live cable on the first strike, sending a shower of sparks raining out across the road. Karen jumped back to escape the blinding fountain, stumbling in her oversized boots and falling to the ground. She landed hard on her ass, dazed and terrified, and scrambled back on her elbows and heels as the sparks showered the ground at her feet.

On the wall above her one end of the severed cable hung loose, the other end arcing a current into a steel box that now glowed blindingly white, forcing her to look away as she shuffled backwards. The ax was still gripped tight in her hands, its edge blackened and scored but otherwise intact, and as far as she could tell she was still in one piece. Her heart was racing and she couldn't catch her breath, but she didn't feel as if she'd taken a jolt from the cable.

Karen's feet cleared the torrent of sparks, and finally she felt safe enough to stop scrambling. She had her back up against the door of a city bus a full lane away from the spitting cables, and as the sharp crackling of the live wire began to die down she finally noticed another sound.

The steady *woomph* of the enormous fans above her seemed to be slowing.

They were spinning to a stop.

She pulled herself to her feet, staring at the blades of the fans as they slowed, and with a cheer of celebration she grabbed the radio and yelled. "Doc, it worked! They're stopping! They're stopping!" She didn't care if he couldn't hear her. She just needed to say it out loud.

Even as she spoke she began to limp back towards the stairwell on legs that trembled like jello, clutching the radio in one hand and the ax in the other. Her heart was still racing and she felt like she wanted to vomit from the strain, but it didn't matter now. In just a couple of minutes she'd be back with Emily, safe and sound.

She was halfway back towards the door when the radio finally broke its long silence. The set crackled in her hand. "… *coming. I can't…*" Ramos' voice barely made it through the interference.

Karen clicked transmit. "What's that, Doc? I didn't catch what you said."

The radio hissed and crackled again. "… *He's… break through… can't hold…*"

Karen scowled at the radio, breaking into an awkward, lop-sided jog. Maybe the signal would improve as she got closer to the control room. "Doc," she panted, already struggling for breath and fighting a stitch, "I still can't hear you. What's wrong?"

Now the signal was more crackle than speech. She could barely pick out a single word. It seemed as if

Ramos was trying to tell her something about a door, but for the life of her she couldn't make sense of anything beyond the interference.

All she knew was that he sounded afraid.

It was only when Karen worked her way across the lanes and back towards the wall of the tunnel that she noticed what was wrong, and her blood turned to ice in her veins as she saw it.

The door to the staircase was hanging wide open.

She'd closed that door. She was *certain* of it. She remembered pushing it closed until she heard the click, because she didn't want to contaminate the staircase any more than she already had.

She stopped in her tracks, ducking down behind the car beside her, her heartbeat thumping in her ears.

"Doc," she whispered into the radio, suddenly aware of how far her voice carried in the tunnel, "what's happening? Is there someone else down there?"

She gripped the ax handle tighter as she waited for a response, her eyes fixed on the open door, and when the crackle returned she jumped so quickly she almost dropped the ax.

Now there were no words. Even when the crackle

faded there was no speech, just… Karen couldn't quite make it out. Heavy breathing? A loud bang?

The next sounds she recognized instantly. They reached down into the depths of her soul, grabbed tight and *squeezed*.

It was Emily's scream.

Followed by a gunshot.

Followed by silence.

CHAPTER THREE
BOTTOM SHELF VODKA

DESPITE THE CHILL in the air Jack was drenched in sweat by the time he'd dragged the bodies to the edge of the forest. It mingled with the dirt and blood that clung to his skin, stinging his red raw eyes as he panted with exertion.

The woman had been easy enough to carry. She'd died close to the tree line, and she didn't weigh all that much, but Warren was a different story. Somehow the old man seemed to have gained weight in death, and it was even more of an effort to drag his bulk across the gas station forecourt than it had been to carry him through the forest.

Jack knew the reason. It was *hope*. Hope that he

might survive had made Warren lighter, but now he was being carried to the grave his every pound weighed heavy on Jack's shoulders. By the time he finally set the old man down beside the body of the woman he barely had the energy to gather the rocks he'd need to cover them.

He knew he really didn't have the time to spare for this little ritual. He knew he should be sprinting towards Emily as fast as his legs would carry him, but... well, it just didn't feel right to leave these people where they'd fallen. He couldn't bear the thought of leaving their bodies out in the open to be scavenged by wildlife. He owed them what little dignity he could offer, even if it cost his time he didn't have.

Hell, he owed Warren his life. Without his help Jack knew he would have died in Seattle. He would have been stranded at the airfield, and even if he'd managed to find a working car he'd have been snarled up in the traffic trying to escape the city. He'd seen those endless tailbacks jamming up the roads. God knows how he would have escaped ahead of the nuke that must surely have hit by now.

As for the woman, her name was Janice. Jack had gone looking for a shovel in the gas station, hoping to be able to bury the bodies, but instead he'd found a stack of old bills and personal letters behind the counter.

She was Janice Fremantle of Tiller, Oregon. She had a long overdue phone bill, a subscription to a monthly woodworking magazine, a daughter up in Portland and a grandson on the way. He'd seen the sonogram pinned up on the wall behind the counter, and he just knew Janice had put it there in the hope that customers might ask about it. He knew that her heart must have damn near burst with joy as she told them about the little boy she'd soon hold in her arms.

And it was Jack's fault that little boy would have to grow up without his grandma.

He'd tried to lie to himself. He'd tried to convince himself that it was Janice's fault for pulling the shotgun. If she'd just stayed calm she'd still be alive and well, but no matter how many times he repeated it as he gathered rocks to cover the bodies he couldn't convince himself.

Of course she'd pulled a gun. He'd limped up to her rural gas station in the middle of the night, miles from anywhere and without a car, his suit torn and bloodied, rambling on about some skydiving accident and an injured friend. Hell, if Jack had found himself in her position he'd have pulled the trigger without a second thought. Without a *first* thought.

Shame gnawed at him as he placed the stones carefully over the bodies, and as Janice slowly vanished from sight Jack played the last hour in his head over and over again, imagining how tragedy could have been averted if he'd just been thinking more clearly. He wished he'd taken Warren's gun from his holster. He wished he hadn't left him alone, delirious and confused. He wished he'd done a million things differently if it meant this woman could still be breathing. If it meant Warren might still be alive. If it meant he didn't have to face the road

When the bodies were finally covered Jack crouched down beside the cairns and took a moment to say a prayer, but he didn't really know how to do it. He hadn't prayed in years. He didn't know the right words, and what began as a prayer quickly turned into an apology. He apologized for what he'd done, for who he was, for everyone he'd failed, until eventually it felt like there were no more words left to say.

When it was over he wiped his eyes on his sleeve and trudged back into the gas station, Boomer trailing disconsolately beside him, and he rifled through Janice's mail until he found a blank piece of paper and a pen.

He explained what had happened in as much detail as he could squeeze onto the page. He apologized to Warren's sons, and to Janice's daughter and unborn grandson, and he signed off with his name, address and phone number, for what little good it would do. The apartment probably didn't even exist any more, but the address might help one of the family members track him down if they wanted to press charges. He'd take the blame, gladly. He wouldn't shirk responsibility. He knew better than most that grieving families needed somewhere to go with their anger, and he'd happily be the punching bag.

When the last word had been written he propped the note against the register. Maybe the police would find it when this was all over.

The store was dark, barely lit by the moonlight creeping through the shattered window, but there was just enough illumination for Jack to make out what was on the shelves. He whispered another apology – to both God and Janice – as he moved through the store stuffing his pockets with bags of peanuts, strips of jerky and a couple of water bottles. When he finally reached the counter he paused, staring at what he found sitting on a shelf beneath it.

He knew he shouldn't. He knew he didn't have the time for this, but almost as if it were a simple reflex he watched his hand reach down and pull out the glass bottle tucked in beside a stack of ledgers. Even as he wrapped his hand around the neck he realized he was already running the justifications through his head, testing them out to find the one that would best temper the shame.

You've earned this, Jack.

If there was ever a day you needed a drink, it's today.

It's medicinal. You'll be able to reach Emily faster if you dull the pain in your body.

Come on, everyone drinks at a wake. Warren would have wanted you to take a drink for him.

The last one was the winner.

It was too dark to read the label on the bottle, but as soon as he spun off the cap he got an dizzying whiff of the contents. Some kind of vodka, bottom shelf by the harsh odor. It smelled like the kind of booze designed to be drowned in Coke and numbed with ice, for people who didn't care for the taste but didn't want to remember their name come midnight.

That suited Jack just fine. He'd never been picky when it came to alcohol. After the last few hours he'd knock back gasoline if someone offered it in a shot glass.

He lowered himself to a rickety wooden stool behind the counter, his fist wrapped tight around the neck of the bottle, and he sighed as he realized he'd already made his peace with what was about to happen. Jack was a drunk, but he wasn't stupid. He'd been here a thousand times before, and he knew that once he'd taken that first sip he wouldn't stop until he could see clear daylight through the bottom.

He brought the bottle to his lips and tipped it back, bracing himself for the rough burn of cheap vodka at the back of his throat. The first belt was always the roughest.

And then he stopped. He lowered the bottle and looked towards the doorway, his lips wet but his throat dry.

Boomer was standing framed in the moonlight, her head hanging low. She padded slowly to his side, and when she finally reached him she stopped, looked up and let out a whine so mournful that Jack felt tears prick at his eyes.

"You miss him, don't you?" he asked, setting the

bottle on the counter and reaching down to scratch Boomer behind the ears.

The dog whined again, resting her head softly in Jack's lap.

"Yeah, me too, buddy."

He reached into a pocket for a bag of nuts, and as he tore open the foil Boomer began to perk up. She raised her head and snuffled at the bag, and when Jack pulled out a handful she attacked them with gusto, her sadness at losing her friend forgotten for the moment.

"You like those, do you?" he asked, tossing a nut into his mouth. Boomer licked her chops and gazed longingly at the bag, panting as Jack shook out another handful. As soon as he opened his palm she dove in, licking the salt from his fingers before turning her attention back to the bag.

"Sorry, that's it," Jack shrugged, shaking the empty bag upside down. "You cleaned me out."

Boomer whined, tilting her head to one side.

Jack pulled out his phone and called up the compass app, his greasy fingers smearing the screen. "I'll tell you what, though," he said, peering at the screen until he figured out which way was south, "if you want to come with me I've got a few more bags."

He pulled one from his pocket and shook it. "What do you say? You wanna stay here, or do you still wanna come with me and meet my little girl?"

He raised himself to his feet and made his way across the room to the doorway, the bottle forgotten on the counter.

"It's your call, girl. Entirely up to you."

He shook the bag again, and as he walked out onto the forecourt Boomer padded to the door. She looked over toward Warren's cairn and then back to Jack, torn between following the snacks and staying by her master's side.

"Totally up to you," Jack repeated, still shaking the bag as he walked. "I'm not pushing you either way."

Now he reached the road. A few dozen more yards and the asphalt would curve around the bend, hiding him in the trees. Still Boomer stood at the gas station door, her head low to the ground, whining unhappily at the choice she had to make.

Jack smiled, pulling from his pocket a vacuum packed strip of jerky, and when he pulled away the wrapping Boomer immediately stood to attention and panted excitedly.

"I'm not making the decision for you," he called back, taking a bite out of the dried meat as he walked.

Now the trees began to close in around him once more, and beneath the canopy the moonlight tried and failed to break through. The gas station behind him began to slip out of view.

And then came a bark, and another, and in the silence of the forest Jack heard the pad of Boomer's feet on the asphalt. She appeared beside him at a run, skidding to a halt and looking up at the treat in his hand.

"What, you want this?" he asked, pointing to the jerky.

Boomer whined, licking her chops, and when Jack lowered it within reach she barely stopped to chew. The jerky vanished down her throat in an instant, and while she was slobbering over it Jack began to walk again.

He'd only gone ten steps before Boomer returned to his side, keeping pace. "You're gonna come along for the ride, huh?" Boomer looked up at him and let out a bark.

"Well, OK, you can come if you really want to, but it's not all peanuts and jerky, understand? That's just a treat because we're sad about Warren. As soon as we find Emily you're back on the healthy stuff, you got me? I'm not gonna let you get fat."

Boomer just panted.

"You'll love Emily, I promise. She'll play with you all the time. Karen… well, Karen maybe not so much. Karen might try to make you eat broccoli."

Boomer let out a whine, padding away ahead of him.

"I know, buddy, I know," he replied, speeding up to keep pace. "I hate it too."

•▼•

CHAPTER FOUR
AX TO A GUNFIGHT

KAREN LEAPED DOWN the steps three at a time, almost turning her ankle in the clumsy work boots as she rounded the bends, but she didn't have time to worry about injury. The sound of the gunshot played over and over in her head, and it was all she could do to keep herself from imagining what she'd find when she reached the bottom of the stairs.

She couldn't remember if Emily's scream had stopped at the same moment the gun had fired. It had all happened so fast she couldn't keep it straight in her head, but her imagination was running faster than she was. The more she thought about it the more she was certain her little girl's scream had been silenced by the shot.

She pushed the terrible thought from her mind, turning the final corner and throwing herself down the last flight of steps. Now she was dripping with sweat in the heavy jacket, and she knew she was inhaling the dust that had settled on it by the lungful, but she didn't care. She couldn't take the time to pull it off.

Below her the bottom of the staircase came into view, and she finally she forced herself to slow down. She could hear her own panting breath echoing off the walls, and the clomp of her boots against the stone sounded deafening. With a superhuman effort she managed to resist the urge to sprint the final hallway to the office door.

At the foot of the staircase she saw a pool of what looked like vomit dripping down the last few steps, thick and bile green. She skirted past it cautiously, ducking down to get a view of the corridor beyond, dreading what she'd find.

The door was open at the end of the hallway, swung back on its hinges and hanging loose, and even from the far end of the corridor Karen could see that the wood around the handle was splintered. Someone had forced it open.

She moved closer, biting her lip to keep from calling Emily's name, and as the sound of low voices crept out from the office ahead she forced herself to stop in her tracks. The fabric of the jacket and pants rustled as she walked, and she was certain that anybody in the office would hear her coming from a mile away.

With exaggerated care she slipped herself out of the high vis clothing and set it down in a heap on the floor, leaving her stripped down once again to her underwear and boots, and then she took the grip of the ax in her hand and brought it up to her shoulder, ready to swing.

She approached the door slowly, struggling to control her breathing, straining to make out the voices in the office beyond.

"Just settle down, OK?"

That sounded like Ramos, his voice slow, steady and soothing.

"We can deal with this, understand? I'm a doctor. I can help you, but first you have to help me. Why don't you start by telling me your name?"

Another voice emerged, this one louder. On edge. Panicked.

"It's... my name is Jared. What's happening to me?

Did… did you do this to me?"

"No, Jared," replied Ramos, struggling to keep his voice steady. "It was the bomb. Do you remember the bomb? It… it made you sick. You understand what I'm telling you? The radiation from the bomb has made you sick. That's why you're feeling so confused right now. You have a high fever, and I need to bring it down to help you get better. You just need to put the gun down and let me help. Do you think you can do that for me, son?"

For a moment Karen could only hear breathing, but then the newcomer yelled out, his voice terrifyingly vicious. "*Don't come closer!* I'll shoot her! I swear to God I'll shoot her right in the head if you take one more step."

When he fell silent a new sound arose, this one much softer. It was weeping, muffled and low, and Karen didn't need more than a moment to recognize the voice as Emily's. She gripped the ax handle tighter, clenching her jaw as tears began to well at her eyes.

Ramos spoke again. "OK, Jared, I'm going to stay right here until you tell me different. I won't come a step closer, OK?"

Karen silently lowered herself to the ground, heart

thumping in her throat as she crept towards the door. She needed to see what was going on in the room, but she knew that if the man saw her there was a chance he might–

No! Don't think about that, she scolded herself. She knew it would do her no good to imagine what Jared might do to Emily if he was provoked. She took a deep breath, pressed her cheek against the door frame and peered around.

Ramos was standing on the far side of the room, dressed in a pair of gray sweatpants and a t-shirt a couple sizes too small, holding out his hands palms forward as if he were trying to calm a wild animal. Halfway between him and Karen was the newcomer, Jared, his back to the door.

Jared was a tall, skinny man dressed in cargo shorts and a loud Hawaiian shirt, his shoulder length blond hair thin and straggly. Beneath his knees the skin of his legs was bright red, as if sunburned, but Karen looked beyond the legs.

In front of him was Emily. He was holding her above the ground, his pink arm wrapped around her throat, and in his other hand... in his other hand he held a gun against her head.

Karen almost growled. The rage was visceral,

uncontrollable. She raised herself from the ground and squeezed the ax handle so tight it felt like her knuckles might burst through the skin, but as she stood Ramos finally noticed her from the other side of the room. He kept his eyes on Jared, but he firmly shook his head and held up both hands.

"We'll all just stay exactly where we are, OK? None of us will move a muscle. I don't want to see anyone get hurt. This will all be over soon. *Understand?*" He was looking directly at Jared, but it was obvious that the message was intended for Karen.

She stood back, her fists clenched white against the ax handle, tears in her eyes. She wanted nothing more than to run up behind the bastard holding her daughter and bury the ax in the back of his head. She wanted to crack open his skull and watch the light fade from his eyes just for *daring* to lay a finger on her little girl. She wanted him to suffer a lifetime of agony for every second of fear he'd caused Emily, but somehow she managed to hold the anger at bay. Ramos seemed to have a plan, and she had to trust that he knew what he was doing.

"Why don't you point the gun at me, son?" Ramos suggested quietly. "Come on, there's no reason to scare the girl. Go on, it's OK. You can point it at me."

Karen couldn't believe what she was hearing. *This* was his plan?

She watched open mouthed as the man raised the gun hesitantly from Emily, and as he leveled it at Ramos' chest she was overcome with guilt as a thought slipped into her mind unbidden.

At least if he kills someone it'll be Ramos, not Emily.

She couldn't believe she'd allowed that thought to bubble up. Of course she *believed* it. There wasn't a mother alive who wouldn't happily sacrifice a town full of people just to keep her child from skinning their knee, but they knew they were never supposed to consciously think it. It was supposed to stay deep down, an instinct rather than a fully formed thought, because even though every parent secretly felt the same it was still too shameful and monstrous a truth to admit, even to yourself.

"That's good," said Ramos, somehow managing to keep his composure as Jared pointed the gun square at his chest. "That's real good. Now how about you let go of the girl and take a seat. Your arm's gotta be hurting holding her up like that. It's OK. Remember, you've got the gun pointed at me. You're safe, OK? You can just let the girl go and rest while we figure this out. Go ahead, son."

Karen watched as Jared took a slow step back. He did seem to be struggling a little under Emily's weight. She ducked quickly behind the door frame as he turned to look at the chair behind him, and she pressed her head against the wall and listened until she heard the sound of wood creaking. He'd taken a seat.

"I'm not letting the girl go," Jared said. "I'm… You gotta fix me, but I'm not letting her go." He was slurring his words now. A moment ago his voice had been full of anger and energy, but now he sounded drunk.

"That's fine, Jared. As long as you keep the gun trained on me you can do whatever you want. You're in charge here." Ramos had dropped his voice low, almost to a whisper. He sounded a little like Jack back in the old days, back when he used to tell bedtime stories to Emily and Robbie, his deep, quiet voice soothing them to sleep. "We're gonna get you all fixed up, son. You just relax. There's nothing to worry about any more."

Karen peered around the door frame again, and now she saw the man leaning back in the chair. He still had a firm grasp on Emily, but now her feet were touching the floor. The pressure was off her throat, and the grip seemed looser. Even the gun...

What the hell?

Karen watched as the barrel of the gun began to slowly drift down. First it slipped away from Ramos' chest, and he continued to speak in a soothing voice as it ran down his legs. He held up a hand again, urging Karen to stay back, and as the barrel finally began to point towards the ground he started to move forward. Just a couple of steps at a time, like a kid playing grandma's footsteps.

Jared was falling asleep!

Still Ramos crept forward. He was halfway across the room now, maybe a half dozen steps from the chair. In a few more seconds he'd be standing in front of him, and he could reach down and–

The grip around Emily's neck suddenly loosened, and Emily realized she could slip her head out carefully from beneath it. Ramos raised a finger to his lips, looking at the little girl with wide, warning eyes, urging her to be quiet, but Karen noticed the problem before he did.

Emily couldn't hold up his arm. She'd managed to lift it high enough to slip out from his grip, but now she was trembling under the weight. Any second now she'd have to drop it, and when she did…

The moment came, and Karen pushed off the door frame and launched herself forward. As Emily dropped his arm Jared suddenly jolted awake, confused and agitated. He raised the gun with a snap, pointing it once again towards Ramos' chest as he yelled out.

"*What? What have you done to me?*"

Jared squeezed the trigger in the same instant Karen swung the ax. It came down from her shoulder in a clumsy arc, and she felt it connect with his skull at the exact same moment the flash burst from the barrel of the gun.

The ax was the wrong way around. Karen caught the man a blow to the ear with the handle, not the blade, and rather than bury itself in his skull it only knocked him off balance, sending his arm flying up and to the left.

But it was enough to save the Doc. As the barrel flashed the gun shifted away from his chest. The bullet zipped past him, catching him in the arm, and he tumbled forward onto his attacker before he had time to get off another shot.

Beneath Ramos' weight Jared fell out of the chair, the gun sliding across the floor, and Karen reached out and tugged Emily clear as Ramos pushed himself up and tried to rain blows on the newcomer.

He'd drawn back his fist for the first punch before he realized it wouldn't be necessary. Beneath him Jared lay rigid, his arms and legs locked out straight, his body convulsing as if a current was passing through it.

"What's happening?" Karen demanded, pulling Emily close.

Ramos rolled off the man and grabbed his arm, pressing down on the patch of blood spreading out across the sleeve of his t-shirt. "It's OK! Don't touch him." He gasped, struggling for breath like a asthmatic at the finish line of a marathon, but he managed to hold up his hand. "Just… just stay back. He's not a threat any more."

Almost as soon as Ramos spoke Jared proved his words to be true. With a final jerk he coughed, a stream of pink frothy blood drooling down his cheek, and a moment later he fell silent and still.

Karen clutched Emily in a tight hug, ignoring the pain in her chest, and her daughter sobbed as she pressed her face against her mom's bare shoulder.

"It's OK, pumpkin, it's OK. He can't hurt you now. Mommy's here." She looked to Ramos. "Doc, what the hell happened? Who was he?"

Ramos panted. "That," he said, baring his teeth to hold back the pain, "is what I hope doesn't happen to you."

Karen shook her head, confused. "What do you mean?"

Ramos nodded to the body, the frothy blood mingling with a stream drying beneath his nose. "Acute radiation sickness," he managed to wheeze. "He was outside too long."

Finally Karen was thinking clearly enough to notice Ramos' injury. The blood had spread to a patch a couple of inches across now, and from the look on his face he was in terrible pain.

"My God, Doc, we have to get you fixed up. What should I do?"

Ramos shook his head, speaking through clenched teeth. "He only clipped me. It's just a graze, I'll live," he panted. "Wash. *Now*. You don't want to end up dying like him."

Karen stared at the spreading patch of blood. "But Doc, we have to get you– "

"It might already be too late for you," he said, raising his injured arm and pointing to the bathroom. "Go! Now!"

"But Doc, we have to– "

"*For God's sake, Karen, look at your hands!*"

Karen let go of Emily and held up her hands, and as soon as she saw them she felt a wave of nausea and dread. They were bright pink and swollen, dry and cracked, ending in a sharp line at her wrists where the skin returned to creamy white. It took her a moment to make the connection, but when she did she stared down at the body on the floor.

It was the fallout. Wherever the air outside had touched the skin it had burned her, and now she realized the same thing had happened to the man's legs. That was why his exposed skin glowed pink. Now she felt the pain in her hands, the throbbing sting of a bad sunburn, and she realized she felt it in her face, too.

"Doc…" She gingerly touched her face, her fingers trembling. Even the lightest touch felt like the drag of fingernails against her skin.

"*What's happening to me?*"

•▼•

CHAPTER FIVE
WITH THAT WILD BEAST?

BY THE THIRD hour on the road Jack glared at Boomer with undisguised envy. He was jealous of the way she casually padded along beside him as if this were just a pleasant walk in the woods, occasionally wandering over to sniff an interesting tree or scoop up a branch in her slobbering jaws. The miles seemed to have no effect on her. She looked like she could keep walking all the way to Modesto.

Jack, on the other hand…

"Hold up a second, girl," he called out, wincing as he lowered himself to the ground at the side of the road. The asphalt was slick with rain and mud, but he'd long since stopped worrying about the state of his clothes. A muddy ass was far from the top of the list of his priorities.

"*Ow ow ow*, oh Jesus," he whispered, groaning as he picked at the laces of his once shiny black Oxfords. "How are you doing this, Boomer?" At the sound of her name the lab wandered back towards him, tilting her head as if to ask *what's up?*

"Ten miles. We must have walked ten freaking miles without seeing a single car, and you still look fresh out of the shower. And look at me," he said, slipping his shoe carefully over his raw heel and rolling down a dress sock. "Look at this damned blister. It's almost a second foot!"

The blister on Jack's heel was translucent and weeping, a stinging flap of skin rubbing against the angry wound where it had burst and broken away. He clenched his teeth as he carefully rolled the sock back on, and when he moved to his other foot he didn't even bother to check it. He knew it was just as bad without looking, so he just slipped off his shoe and left the sock alone.

"I don't suppose you have a band aid on you?" he asked, as Boomer poked her nose inside his suit jacket. "No? Not even a little one?" She tried to push her way into his pocket, searching for the snacks hidden within. "Of course not. You're just a damned freeloader, aren't you?" He pushed her head away and grabbed her affectionately around the neck. "A big, furry freeloader. You only want me for my snacks, don't you?"

He reached into his pocket and pulled out another piece of jerky. "You may be able to walk ten miles on those paws, but they're no good for tearing open plastic, right? Admit it. Hands beat paws." He split open the pack and tore off a piece of jerky.

"OK, go get it." He tossed it far ahead, calling after her as she raced off to find it. "I'll catch up." He looked down at his ruined feet and sighed. "Just as soon as I get a new body."

Ten miles. Back home you couldn't walk ten miles without stumbling on a dozen gas stations and a couple of strip malls, but that sort of distance was nothing in Oregon. Here it was just a short stroll through the woods. For all Jack knew it could be another fifty miles to the nearest hamlet, and in his heart of hearts he knew he'd drop dead long before that. Even without the blisters he just didn't have the legs for more than another hour or two. He needed to rest his aching feet, eat a meal and grab some real sleep. He wasn't built for this.

The problem wasn't that he was out of shape. Considering it had been the best part of two decades since he'd last run track he was impressively slim, but his thirty two inch waist wasn't maintained through exercise and healthy living. His lats showed because he often forgot to eat, and whiskey doesn't have all that many calories, and his toned stomach didn't come from crunches. It was the result of crouching over countless toilets, heaving up the remnants of the last night's excesses. He hadn't jogged more than a mile in three years, and it showed in his aching calves and ragged breath.

He tied his shoes together by their laces, hanging them around his neck before he pulled himself to his feet, and with an exhausted sigh he reluctantly began to plod after Boomer. She was the only thing keeping him going now, setting the pace and dragging him along for the ride.

It only took a few steps before Jack's socks were soaked, and he realized it had probably been a mistake to remove his shoes. Ten minutes from now his cold, wet feet would be driving him crazy. He'd be praying for warmth, kicking himself for being so dumb.

Still, the pain was gone now that the heels of his

shoes were no longer scraping against his blisters, and already he could feel his pace quicken without the wincing hobble holding him back. Now, with the cool night breeze at his back and a soft, gentle slope in the road, he found himself breaking into a slow jog. More of a barely controlled stumble, if he was honest with himself, but however he'd describe it he was moving much more quickly without the constant sawing of leather against his heels.

"Boomer," he called out, his voice sounding eerily loud in the heavy silence of the surrounding forest. "Boomer? Where are you, girl?"

There was no response. She can't have gone far, he thought. His throwing arm wasn't that strong, so she'd only had to run a couple dozen yards to find the jerky. Even if she'd bolted off into the trees on whatever mysterious errand labradors take on she should still be well within earshot.

"*Boomer!*" He called a little louder, and again he was met with deathly silence. He brought his fingers to his lips, pursed around them and let out a piercing whistle.

It was so loud it surprised even Jack, lingering over the forest for seconds after he stopped. Every dog for ten miles must have pricked up its ears at the shrill whistle, but still there was no response from Boomer. It was as if she'd vanished from the face of the earth.

And then, finally, a sound broke the silence, but it wasn't the dog.

It was an answering whistle.

Almost without thinking Jack scurried into the shadows at the side of the road, the hairs on his neck standing on end. He crouched in the darkness, scanning up and down the road for signs of movement, but with the breeze rustling through the trees there was nothing *but* movement. Both the road and the forest floor seemed to shift unceasingly in the swaying, dappled moonlight. A dozen armed men could be standing a stone's throw from him and he'd never know it.

Jack felt exposed and vulnerable, and for the first time since he'd walked away from the gas station he felt his heart pound in his chest. He'd expected cars, not walkers. It had never occurred to him that someone else might be on foot out here, stalking the forest in the dead of night.

Would they be friendly, or a threat? Surely it was too much to hope that anyone out here tonight might be a friend. It wasn't as if he was going to stumble on a scout pack toasting s'mores over a campfire. Much more likely it would be…

He shook his head, stopping that train of thought the moment the word *Deliverance* popped into his mind.

"Don't be stupid, Jack," he muttered, trying to calm himself with the sound of his own voice. "You're in Oregon. It's probably some hipster kid in $300 hiking boots."

As he convinced himself of his overreaction he felt his confidence begin to return, and as he stepped out from the shadows he chided himself that his first thought had been to hide. What did he have to be afraid of? After all, he thought, reaching into his pocket for the comforting heft of Warren's pistol, it's not like he was helpless. He knew the gun was empty, but nobody he bumped into on the road would know that at a glance. All they'd see would be an armed man ready to defend himself. They'd turn and run as soon as–

The whistle came again, loud, shrill and close. It seemed to be coming from all around him, and as it echoed through the trees he felt the fear bubble up once more.

"Hello?" he called out, consciously dropping his voice an octave. "Is somebody there?"

He listened carefully, and over the rustle of the leaves in the trees he'd swear he could hear a voice, oddly muffled but somewhere nearby. He gripped the gun a little tighter.

"I can't hear you! Do you need help?"

The voice returned, this time much clearer. It was a man's voice, high pitched and panicked, and it seemed to be coming from straight ahead, just a little way down the road.

"Please call off your dog!"

Jack broke into a run, racing in sodden feet down the gentle slope. Up ahead there was a soft kink in the road, a long bend verged by red alder trees swaying in the breeze, and as Jack began to round it he saw a vehicle parked by the side of the road a hundred yards ahead, a Civic with the driver's door hanging open.

The whistle came again and again in quick bursts, and then the panicked voice returned. "*Please!* I can't hold on much longer!"

The voice was coming from the edge of the forest beside the car, and as Jack approached he finally saw Boomer standing at the foot of an alder, pawing at the trunk, looking up into the branches and yapping out curious barks.

"Boomer!" Jack yelled out. "Heel!"

She ignored him. It was clear that Warren hadn't trained her well, but at least she knew enough to run towards food. Jack pulled the last bag of peanuts from his jacket and shook it, and the dog came running.

"Hold her back!" The muffled voice cried out as Boomer reached Jack and began to leap excitedly around him.

Jack finally caught sight of the man, a middle aged professorial type in a rough tweed jacket that looked to be caught up on a half dozen low branches, leaving him looking like a marionette suspended by its strings. He clung desperately to the narrow trunk of the tree like a squirrel, his legs wrapped around it and his cheek pressed up against the bark.

"Are you OK?" asked Jack. "Are you hurt?"

The man was breathing heavily, clearly struggling. "Do you have that thing under control?" For the first time the voice was clear enough that Jack noticed an English accent, clipped and precise.

Jack looked down at Boomer, staring up at the peanuts with wide, covetous eyes, panting as she waited for the treat. He reached down and took her by the collar. "Settle down, Boomer. Umm, yeah, I've got hold of her." He still couldn't figure out what was going on. "Do you need help or something? What are you doing up there?"

From the tree came a long scraping sound, and in the mottled white of the moonlight Jack watched with amusement as the man gracelessly slid down the trunk, his jacket pulling up over his shoulders as it clung to the branches. He slid in fits and starts, falling a few inches at a time before eventually he lost his grip, and he dropped the final few feet and landed in an ungainly pile in the leaf litter, his clothing in disarray.

He pushed a pair of horn rimmed glasses up the bridge of his nose, checked to make sure Boomer wasn't running for him, and then scrambled back towards his car on hands and knees.

"*Wait!*" Jack yelled as the man leaped through the driver's door, slamming it behind him. "We're stranded! Please, can you give us a ride?"

The man cracked his window an inch and looked out at Boomer with an expression of sheer horror. "With that wild beast? You must be insane!"

Jack looked down at Boomer, sniffing innocently at the bag of peanuts, impatiently waiting for him to open them. "Beast?" He raised an eyebrow. "She's just a labrador. She's like… like a furry toddler."

The man curled his lip in disgust. "You say that like it's a *good* thing." He shivered with revulsion. "That monster came bounding out of the darkness like the Hound of the bloody Baskervilles just as I was… taking a comfort break. I almost had a heart attack! Your dog, sir, could have spelled the end of me!"

Jack stifled a laugh. The man was clearly one of the *special people*, not quite on planet earth with everyone else, but he couldn't afford to offend him. He had a car, and Jack's feet wouldn't take too much more walking.

"I'm very sorry, sir. I'm sure that must have been quite, umm… quite alarming for you." He took a step towards the station wagon, careful to keep a hold of Boomer's collar. "I'm Jack, and this is Boomer. I'm sure she didn't mean any harm. She's just a friendly dog. I swear to you she wouldn't hurt a fly."

"Garside," the man replied reluctantly, his courtesy just about winning out over his pink-faced indignation. "Douglas Garside. And you should keep that thing on a leash all the same. Dogs should not be allowed to run wild, scaring the wits out of innocent people."

"You're absolutely right," Jack agreed with a firm

diplomatic nod. "I'll be sure to keep her on a tight leash in the future, but in the meantime we're stranded out here. If I tie her up securely and keep her well away from you could we please get a ride into the next town? We've been walking for hours, and I really need to to get home to my daughter.

Garside looked down at the dog with a hateful expression, then back up to Jack.

"Even if I wanted that thing shedding hairs all over my car it would do you no good. I've broken down. I've been waiting here for a tow truck or a Good Samaritan for several hours, but I haven't seen a single vehicle on this godforsaken road, and I haven't been able to get a signal on my blasted mobile."

"Your car broke down?" A thought occurred to Jack, and the moment it did he kicked himself for not putting the pieces together hours ago. "What happened? Was it the electrics?"

Garside nodded, narrowing his eyes. "Well, yes. It seemed as if everything just went haywire in an instant. All the lights lit up on my dashboard, and then the whole thing went dead. How could you possibly know that?"

Jack laughed out loud. Now it all made sense. That's why Warren's plane had fallen out of the sky.

It's why the lights had been out at the gas station. It's why Janice had been struggling to start the generator, and why there had been no cars on the road since he'd first stepped onto the asphalt three or four hours ago.

"It's not just your car," he said, shaking his head. "It's everything. *Everything's* dead."

●▼●

CHAPTER SIX
GRAY'S ANATOMY

KAREN WATCHED WITH tearful eyes as vomit and dirty gray water sluiced down the drain in the center of the floor, carrying with it the radioactive dust that seemed to have found its way to every inch of her body. The tepid water felt scalding against her inflamed skin, and she wept with pain as Ramos scrubbed her with a wet dishcloth that felt like a steel wool scouring pad.

"We're almost done, Karen," Ramos assured her. "I'm sorry, I know it hurts. It'll all be over soon. Just hold still a little longer."

She was naked, crouched down on all fours with the floor tiles biting into her trembling knees, but she didn't care. There was no room in her head for self consciousness. The pain was too great to think about anything but the water cascading over her each time the Doc tipped his bucket, and what little space was left was occupied by fear. Fear that she'd end up like the man lying dead in the next room, raving incoherently through her final moments as the sickness stripped her sanity away.

Finally, after what felt like an agonizing eternity, the faucet stopped running and Ramos announced that she was as clean as she'd ever get. Karen fell sideways with relief, curled in the fetal position on the cool tiles, struggling to hold off the waves of nausea that flowed through her every few moments. She felt like she'd been beaten up. *Everything* hurt.

The door back to the office cracked open an inch. Karen knew it was Emily coming to check on her, but she ignored the quiet, concerned voice as her daughter asked Ramos what was happening, and she ignored Ramos himself as he stepped over to the door and whispered that mommy was resting before he closed it in Emily's face. She didn't have the energy to face her little girl, nor worry about her fear.

"How are you feeling?" Ramos asked, crouching into a squat beside her. "How's the nausea?"

Karen groaned. She didn't want to speak for fear that it would bring on another bout of vomiting, but she struggled to get the words out. "Bad. I feel like I'm dying. *Am* I dying?" She gagged, holding it back with a deep breath. "Be honest with me, Doc."

Ramos ignored the question. "Can you follow my finger?" He moved his forefinger back and forth in front of her face. She did her best to keep up, but it was hard to concentrate. "That's good. Now, can you remember the date of Emily's birthday?"

Karen frowned. "What? Why?"

"Emily's birthday," Ramos repeated. "What's the date?"

"It's…" Dredging her memory felt like fighting through a cloud of cotton candy. Everything felt… fuzzy, but it finally came to her. "It's April fifth."

"Good, good," said Ramos, speaking in a soothing tone. "And can you tell me where you are right now?"

She struggled up to her elbows, fighting off the spins that hit her as her head left the floor. "I'm in a bathroom by an office under a tunnel on the bridge out of San Francisco, Doc. I'm stark naked and I feel like I'm gonna throw up all over you. Why are you asking me these questions?"

Ramos replied patiently. "I'm just trying to assess

your faculties, Karen. Trust me, this is important." He touched the back of his hand against her forehead. "How's your head? Do you have a headache or migraine? Any kind of visual impairment? Maybe you're seeing spots or colors? Anything like that?"

"I... I don't know. I guess my head hurts a little, and everything looks a bit... swimmy. But are you surprised? I must have hit it a dozen times in the last couple of hours." Now she dragged herself up into a seated position, shuffling on her ass until her back was against the wall. She could breathe a little easier now she was upright.

"Seriously, Doc," she said, holding back tears. "I want you to be brutally honest. Don't sugarcoat it. Am I dying?"

Ramos took a seat beside her, shifting into place with a sharp intake of breath as the sleeve of his t-shirt shifted across the graze the bullet had scored into his arm. "No sugar coating?"

"No." Karen shook her head. "I want to know. Please don't lie to me."

Ramos nodded. "OK. OK, here it is. I just don't know."

Karen felt her stomach flip, but this time it wasn't the nausea.

"You should understand that this is far from an exact science," Ramos continued, "and without a lab there's just no way to know for sure, but based on your symptoms my best guess is that you got a cumulative dose of radiation in the region of two or three Grays."

"What in hell does that mean?" Karen demanded. "Roentgens, Grays... these are all just meaningless words, Doc."

Ramos fidgeted nervously with his hands, avoiding meeting her eye. "I'm a radiologist, not a radiation oncologist. This really isn't my specialty, but a typical patient undergoing aggressive radiation therapy will be exposed to a dose of two Grays per session. That's... well, I don't want to say the maximum *safe* dose, because it's *not* safe. Two Grays can be fatal, but that's the maximum dose we're willing to risk. Anything above that is... well, it's touch and go."

"And you're saying I got two or three?"

Ramos shook his head firmly. "I'm guessing, just guessing. I want to make that clear. Like I said, this isn't my specialty. I'm just looking at your symptoms and making an educated guess. Your nausea, your headache, the radiation burns, your cognitive impairment... I'm guessing you maybe got a little more than two."

Karen protested. "Cognitive impairment? No! I followed your finger. I answered your questions. I'm thinking clearly, Doc. There's nothing wrong with my brain."

Ramos rested his hand on Karen's shoulder. "Karen, you told me Emily's birthday was April fifth."

"Yes! Yes, April fifth, that's right!"

Ramos sighed. "I'm so sorry to do this to you, Karen, I really am, but I remember the day Emily was born. I was working that day. I remember Jack pulled me out of a consult to hand me a cigar." He took Karen's hand, trying to comfort her. "What I remember clearly was that it was the day after *my* birthday. It was October eighteenth, Karen."

Karen's mouth opened and closed for a moment, her brow knitted in confusion. "April… Yeah, October eighteenth. It was… Oh, God."

She buried her head in her hands, and when she lifted herself back up her eyes were welling with tears. "April fifth was Robbie's birthday. Of *course* Emily was born in October. I *knew* that. Why did I say April?"

"It's OK." Ramos squeezed her shoulder. "Don't worry, it's really OK. A little confusion is expected."

Karen wiped her eyes with the back of her hands. "Expected of what, Doc? What's going to happen to me? Will I end up like that crazy guy out there, barely conscious of where I am?"

Ramos shook his head firmly. "No, absolutely not. I'm guessing that guy was directly exposed to the fallout from the moment of the blast. He got five, ten times your dose, and by his mental state and his seizure I'm guessing he had a severe cerebral edema. He was dead long before he found his way down to us. His body just hadn't figured it out yet."

"So I'm not gonna go crazy?"

"No, you're not gonna go crazy. The confusion you're feeling now is as bad as it'll get, I hope."

"But you still don't know if I'll survive?"

Ramos looked uncomfortable, shifting awkwardly as he carefully framed the answer.

"I'm not an expert on radiation sickness, Karen. I'm sorry I can't hand down the word of God on a stone tablet, but I only studied this stuff for a couple semesters half a lifetime ago. All I remember is that the LD50/60 – that's the dose at which 50% of people will die within 60 days – is something like two and a half Grays. Some people can die with as little as one. Others can survive six."

"So… so what, it's 50/50 whether I'll live or die?"

Ramos blew out his cheeks and shrugged. "Without treatment? Maybe. If you've taken enough damage to your bone marrow your white count will tank, and then…" He didn't want to continue, but he could see from Karen's expression that she wanted the truth, no matter how bleak. He sighed.

"Most people who die from radiation sickness aren't killed by the radiation itself. They're killed by internal bleeding caused by the breakdown of tissue, or by an infection that a weakened immune system can't fight off. It's… it's like AIDS, in a way. The condition itself is just a catalyst. It damages your immune system so badly that you can be taken out by the common cold."

Karen's head dropped. She stared vacantly at the floor, fighting off tears.

"I'm sorry, I…" Ramos awkwardly patted her on the shoulder. "People always told me my bedside manner sucks."

"No, Doc, it's fine," Karen replied, not at all convincingly. "I asked you not to sugarcoat it." She let out a long groan. "Oh, I think I'm gonna throw up. Can you get me some water?" She took a deep, shuddering breath, and then a thought occurred to her. "Wait, is it safe for us to drink water from the faucet?"

Ramos nodded, climbing to his feet. "It'll be safe enough. By the time it reaches the faucet almost all of the fallout will have been filtered out. It's not so dangerous that we have to worry about it." He looked around the bathroom. "Hang on, I need to find a glass for you. Can you give me a minute?"

Karen shook her head. "I'll come with you." Ramos began to protest, but she waved him off. "Doc, I don't want to spend another minute in this room. Can you help me up?"

She held out her hands, and with his help she raised herself on legs that shook like a newborn foal. For a moment she worried she didn't have the energy to stand unaided, but eventually her balance returned enough for her to pull on her underwear and reclaim a fraction of her dignity.

"Oh, Christ, look at me," she gasped, catching sight of herself in the grimy mirror above the basin. From the neck up her skin was bright pink, and so swollen that her eyes were pinched half closed.

"It's not as bad as it looks," Ramos assured her. "It's not much more than a bad sunburn. The redness should fade in a week of so, but we'll keep an eye out for blistering. Try not to scratch if it starts to itch, or you could scar."

Karen almost laughed, but the nausea had stolen her sense of humor. "Itchy skin is pretty far down my list of concerns, Doc, but I'll bear it in mind." She turned away from the mirror. "OK, let's get out of here."

Emily was waiting on the other side of the door as Ramos pulled it open, eyes wide and fearful. She looked like she'd been crying, but the smile returned the moment she saw Karen on her feet.

"*Mommy!*" she squealed, eyes alight with joy. She ran towards Karen for a hug, but Ramos caught her as she swept past him.

"Whoa there. I don't think your mom's ready for bear hugs just yet, Emily. Why don't we let her rest a little, OK?"

Emily fell back, disappointed. "Mommy always gives me a hug when I get sick."

"Of course she does," Ramos smiled. "Hugs are the perfect medicine for kids, but sometimes grownups need a little rest to get better. And water. Shall we go find mommy a drink of water?"

Emily nodded enthusiastically.

"Thank you, pumpkin," Karen said weakly. "I love

you."

"OK," said Ramos, "I think I saw a glass in that break room over there. What do you say you and I go look for it?"

Emily led Ramos by the hand through the door while Karen felt her way over to the office chair, supporting herself on the desks to keep from stumbling. As she lowered herself into the seat she stared at the drops of blood on the empty floor beside it. Ramos must have dragged Jared's body out into the hall before following her to the bathroom.

She found it difficult to grasp just how little time it had taken for the fallout to destroy the man. He'd been out in it... what, no more than an hour or so since the blast? Sixty minutes of exposure, and it had been enough to wreak such damage on his body that his sanity had burned away like a morning mist. Karen had been out for no more than five minutes, but even that may have been enough to sign her death warrant.

What had the Doc said? A 50/50 chance of survival without treatment? She didn't like the sound of those odds.

The break room door swung open, and Emily emerged holding a bottle of mineral water. "Mommy, it's still cold!" She ran over and handed it to Karen, who spun off the cap and greedily chugged half of it before she took a gasping breath.

"Oh, God, that's good. Thank you, pumpkin." She turned to Ramos. "There's a refrigerator?"

"Yeah," Ramos confirmed. "There's not much in the way of food, but we're all set for chilled water and coffee for a while, provided the power holds out. Now I think about it, I'm not sure how the lights are even still on. Do you think there's some kind of generator? I guess there'd have to be, right? To keep the fans running and– "

"Doc," Karen interrupted. She beckoned him closer, lowering her voice so Emily couldn't hear. "What you said earlier about my... my odds? You said that's *without* treatment, right?"

Ramos nodded.

"So what would be the treatment, if I showed up like this at the hospital on a regular day?"

Ramos perched on the edge of the desk beside him and pondered the question.

"Well, I'm no expert, but right away I'd run a blood panel to establish your white count. That'd give me a better idea of the exact radiation dose you absorbed, and how much damage has been done to your bone marrow. I'd probably give you a transfusion and start treatment with granulocyte-colony stimulating factor to boost your white count and strengthen your immune system, and I'd start you on an anti-emetic to deal with the nausea."

He thought about it a little longer. "Oh, and topical treatments to deal with your burns and prevent blistering. That's where an infection would probably sneak through. I'm sure a specialist would have a better idea, but that's about the size of it."

Karen nodded. "And if I got this treatment my odds would be…?"

Ramos pulled a face. "We don't like to handicap these things, Karen. It doesn't work that way."

"Damn it, Doc!" Karen snapped. "Nobody's going to sue you if you get it wrong. I just want an idea, OK?"

"OK, OK. I'd imagine if you got the right treatment, if you didn't get a higher dose than my estimate, and knowing that you're clearly a fighter… yeah, your odds of making it through would be good. I'd expect you to survive."

Karen leaned back in her chair, fighting off another wave of nausea. "And without it, 50/50. I should have stayed in bed this morning."

Behind her eyes the throbbing pressure of a headache was beginning to build. She wasn't sure if it was the radiation or the stress, but either way it felt like a big one. She kneaded the bridge of her nose, groaning.

"Are you really sick, mommy?" Emily took hold of Karen's arm and leaned gently into her shoulder, holding herself back from a full hug.

Karen wrapped her arm around her daughter, drawing her in. "It's OK, honey, I'm just a little bit sick. It's nothing for you to worry about."

Emily sniffled and turned to Ramos. "She said I didn't have to worry when daddy got sick, but he didn't get better."

"Oh, honey," Karen stroked her hair. "It's nothing like that. I just need a little medicine, that's all, but we can't get it right now so we just need to sit tight a while, OK?"

"Can't Doctor Ramos get the medicine? You said Daddy always knew how to get medicine."

Karen almost laughed at what Emily had gleaned from overheard arguments. She must have eavesdropped on a row about Jack faking scripts for Percocet.

"I'm sorry, pumpkin," she said. "Even Doctor

Ramos doesn't know where we can get the medicine I need. All the hospitals are closed right now. We'll go looking for it as soon as– "

"Wait." Ramos interrupted her, scratching his stubble, deep in thought. He suddenly stood bolt upright and crossed the room with a sense of purpose, muttering to himself. "Wait, wait, wait... just hold on a minute." He pulled open the door to the hallway, and without another word he vanished.

"Doc! Where the hell are you going?"

For a couple of minutes Karen stared open mouthed at the door. She had no clue what Ramos was thinking, but she didn't have the energy to chase him. She doubted she could even pull herself out of the chair unless someone rolled a grenade under it.

Eventually the door swung open again, and Ramos reappeared holding his irradiated lab coat gingerly between two fingers. "Sorry, sorry, I didn't mean to scare you." He carefully reached into a pocket and pulled something from it, then tossed the coat as far as he could back out into the hall.

"Sorry, but Emily's right. I *do* know where to get the medicine. Look." He dropped into Karen's lap a sheaf of printed pages, packed from corner to corner with small print that looked like... Karen didn't know what it was, but it all looked vaguely medical in nature.

"That's what the National Guard were evacuating from the hospital before I found you. They cleaned out our medical stores down to the last aspirin. Look, it's all here." He snatched the papers back, flipping the pages. "G-CSF. They have enough Neupogen to replenish your white count a hundred times over. Tetanus vaccine, chlorhexidine, silver nitrate, blood units for all types. They got everything. This," he poked at the list with a finger, "*this* will keep you alive."

Realization dawned on Karen. "They were evacuating this stuff? To the…?" She shook her head. "*No!* Absolutely not, Doc. I won't take Emily there. We'll have to think of something else."

"There *is* nothing else. The safe zone is the only game in town, Karen, and if you don't want to go there you'll have to…" he cupped his hands over Emily's ears, lowering his voice to a harsh whisper. "You'll have to explain to your little girl why her mom has to die before she's out of the damned second grade. Her brother's already gone, and there's no telling if Jack's still alive. Do you really want her to be all alone in the world? You think I can take care of her? I can barely take care of myself." He released Emily, patting her head. "Sorry, honey, just a little grown up talk."

Emily's eyes were full of tears, and she looked up at her mom. "I heard what he was saying. Mommy, are you going to die?" Her lower lip wobbled. "I don't want you to die!" She gripped Karen's arm tight, turning to Ramos with fear in her eyes. "You're not going to let my mommy die, right?"

Ramos shook his head, lowering himself into a crouch before Emily. "No, honey, I'm not going to let her die." He looked up at Karen, ignoring the anger and frustration in her face. "We're going to get her the medicine she needs."

•▼•

CHAPTER SEVEN
AN ACT OF GOD

JACK STARED CURIOUSLY at Douglas Garside's blank, uncomprehending face, wondering just what might have gone wrong with the screwed up internal wiring of the man's mind.

For the life of him he couldn't figure out how the guy ticked. Boomer's appearance had sent him fleeing up a tree in a fit of terror, and when Jack arrived he'd become apoplectic with rage, but when he told the over-excitable Brit about the nuclear blast in the skies above… nothing. Garside accepted the news with polite disinterest, as if Jack had just told him the score of a game in a sport he didn't follow. It was… eerie.

At first Jack wondered if the man might have misunderstood what he was trying to tell him. He'd heard the old joke about the US and England being divided by a common language, and he knew the Brits used their own terms for things like sidewalks and elevators, but surely it wasn't possible that American and British English had diverged so far that a Brit wouldn't understand that a nuke had exploded above his head? Jack tried to explain again using simpler words, looking for an angle that might get through to the man, but once again Garside merely shrugged.

"Well, it was always a matter of time with you lot, wasn't it?" he sighed, as if this were nothing but a casual conversation about the weather. "Always waving your nuclear willy around, poking your nose in where it doesn't belong. I can't say I'm at all surprised that someone finally waggled theirs back."

Jack stared at the man in disbelief. He couldn't grasp how he could be so blasé about a nuclear attack. "You know this happened pretty much directly above us, right?" He pointed a finger straight up. "A nuclear blast. Above us. Right up there."

Garside let out a dry chuckle, peering up into the dark sky. "You know, I always thought Americans all pronounced it 'nucular'. You live and learn." He sniffed. "Anyway, I don't like to get involved in other people's affairs. I'm just a visitor, so I don't suppose it's my place to comment."

He nudged his glasses further up his nose and peered over Jack's shoulder as he bent over the engine bay. "So, have you figured out my car trouble yet?" he asked, in a tone that suggested that as far as he was concerned it was time to move away from nuclear war and on to more important matters.

Jack pushed away from the engine bay and wiped his oily hands on his jacket. "Yeah, I figured out your damned car trouble. See that thing right there?" He snapped, jabbing a finger at the alternator. "It overloaded and fried all your electrics."

Garside tutted. "Bugger. Sounds like an expensive repair."

"And do you know *why* it overloaded, Doug?" Jack asked, testily.

"It's Douglas, if you don't mind," Garside corrected. "I never warmed to Doug. And no, I'm afraid I'm not really *au fait* with the inner workings of cars."

"It overloaded, *Doug*," Jack explained, "because a nuclear bomb exploded a few miles over your head, and it sent a *massive* electromagnetic pulse cascading through the atmosphere, wiping out every power line, vehicle and circuit board for Christ knows how many miles around. Do you understand what I'm telling you? Do you get how serious this is?"

Garside fell silent, staring down with glazed eyes at the engine, deep in thought. His shoulders slumped as he leaned against the car.

Jack coughed and awkwardly averted his gaze, leaving the man to his thoughts. It looked like reality was finally sinking in. Maybe he'd been too hard on him, he thought. It seemed clear to him that Garside was in shock. He'd dealt with the news by shutting down and refusing to face the situation, unable to think clearly and process what happened, but by the stricken expression creeping across his face it looked as if he was finally beginning to grasp the enormity of what was going on.

Eventually Garside stepped away from the car. He took a few paces towards the trees, clasped his hands behind his head and drew a deep breath before letting out a disconsolate sigh.

"My insurance isn't going to cover this repair, is it? I got the fully comprehensive package, but I suppose those cheating buggers will argue it's an act of God, won't they?"

Jack finally lost his patience with the man. "For Christ's sake, Doug!" He stepped back from the car and threw up his hands. "You're acting like it's no big deal that nukes are blowing up above your head! Are you mentally ill, or are you just stupid?"

For a moment Garside seemed to seriously ponder the question. He tilted his head back and looked to the sky above him, then back to Jack before replying in a calm, quiet voice.

"Sir, I'm neither stupid nor mentally ill. I'm just British, and we know a thing or two about keeping a level head in a crisis. Have you never heard of the Blitz?"

Jack glowered at Garside. "You freaked out at the sight of a labrador, Doug. Let's not go overboard with your keep calm and carry on bullshit."

Garside bristled. "It was merely a prudent reaction to an imminent threat, Mr. Archer, and I'm not sure I appreciate your tone."

"You squealed like a stuck pig and climbed a tree," Jack mocked.

He couldn't help himself. He knew he was being cruel. He knew it wasn't Garside's fault that his traumatized mind had taken refuge in triviality rather than address the situation head on, but the man just had a certain punchable quality about him. There was something about his priggish manner that made Jack's fists clench without his brain ever sending the message to his hands. Shock had given him the sort of dim, supercilious arrogance of a man who was too stupid to realize he was stupid, a walking example of the Dunning-Kruger effect, and Jack found it easy to imagine that if he asked Garside when he'd last been punched in the face the answer would come in weeks, not years.

He slammed down the hood, sending Garside into a full body flinch. He tried to take a more conciliatory tone, but he couldn't seem to stop himself from affecting a bumbling English accent just to annoy the man. "If it wouldn't be too much of a bother, old boy, would you mind awfully if I ask you to get behind the wheel and prepare for locomotion?"

Garside broke into a broad smile, either ignoring or completely missing Jack's mocking tone. "You think you can get me moving again?"

Jack shook his head. "No. I think I can get *us* moving. This thing's a stick shift, right?" He noticed Garside's gormless expression, and shifted into his language. "Your car has a manual transmission, am I right?"

"Of course it's a manual," Garside spluttered. "It's only you Americans who like to drive automatics, like some sort of enormous couch on wheels."

Jack ignored the insult. "Good. That means it should be easy enough to push start it without the starter motor." He shoved past Garside, moved to the back of the car and pulled open the rear door. "Up you go, Boomer, go on."

Garside watched in horror as the dog hopped up onto the back seat and immediately began to slobber over the driver's head rest. "I told you I won't have that thing in my car!" he protested, moving towards the door.

Jack blocked his way. "Now here's the deal, Doug. Push starting a car is a two man job. I push, you pop the clutch. You can't do it alone without a big ass hill, and I don't see any around." He pushed closed the rear door with a sense of finality. "So Boomer stays, or she and I walk away. Now get in the damn car, turn on the ignition, shift into second and hold down the clutch until I say so."

Garside began to protest, but when he met Jack's defiant gaze he deflated. His haughty bravado abandoned him and he slouched around to the driver's door, muttering under his breath.

"Glad we got that cleared up," said Jack, moving to the back of the car. "Oh, and one more thing, Doug. When I get this thing moving I want you to stop and wait for me, and leave the engine running. If you try to leave without me Boomer will tear your throat out before you can get out a scream. She's well trained. Do we have an understanding?"

The color drained from Garside's face as he looked through the windshield at Boomer, and Jack forced himself to hold back a smirk. He couldn't imagine what bloodcurdling image Garside had conjured in his mind, but in reality Boomer was snuffling around the footwell, licking the chocolate from a discarded candy bar wrapper.

"I'll stop," Garside nodded, his voice weak. "Just don't let her touch me."

Jack braced himself against the trunk of the car. "Good. Boomer, *sit.*"

The dog lazily climbed up onto the rear seats and rested her muzzle on a headrest, looking through the rear window with an expression Jack had come to recognize as *do you have snacks?*

"Good girl. Now stay there. Doug? Second gear. Handbrake off."

Garside carefully lowered himself into the driver's seat, hunched forward over the wheel to maintain as much distance as possible from the slobbering labrador behind him. "Good boy," he said, before quickly correcting himself. "Sorry, *girl!* Good girl… Please don't bite me."

With slow, exaggerated movements Garside turned the key and shifted into second gear, and he gripped the wheel for dear life as Jack planted his shoulder against the trunk, pushing the car slowly forward with what little strength he could muster.

"Straighten it up," he called out as the Civic veered to the right, further into the undergrowth. "Guide it back to the road."

Jack felt like he was burning through the final few calories of his energy reserves now. The counter was about to hit zero, and despite the chill in the air his forehead beaded with sweat as the car began to creep forward. Every inch was a struggle, but when the tires finally crept onto the smooth asphalt the going got a little easier, and the slight downward slope was a gift for his trembling legs.

Eventually Jack felt the car begin to overtake his feet, and he shifted the pressure from his aching shoulder to his hands. His aching legs moved like pistons, boosting the car a little faster with each push off the asphalt, and after just a few moments he found himself moving at walking pace. "OK, pop the clutch now," he called out.

Nothing happened. Exhaustion burned at his calves.

"Doug, pop the clutch!"

From behind the wheel Garside called out through the half open window. "I don't know what that means!"

Jack groaned. "It means lift your damned foot off the clutch, quickly!"

"Ah, sorry. Righto!"

Jack felt the weight of the car double against his hands as the clutch disengaged and the gearbox pushed back against him. For a moment he feared it would grind to a halt and he'd have to somehow dredge up the energy to start again, but just as it seemed about to roll to a stop the engine coughed, coughed again, and finally came to life.

"It's working!" Garside cried, squeezing the gas and jolting forward, leaving Jack's hands to slip from the trunk. He stumbled forward into a run as the car roared forward, and when Garside slammed on the brakes Jack went barreling into the back of it, his legs trembling and his energy spent. He fumbled his way along the side of the car, yanked open the door and fell into the passenger seat with a relieved sigh.

"Drive," he ordered, pointing out the windshield.

"Where to?" Garside asked, as if the narrow country road offered a range of options.

"Doesn't matter. Just… forward. South. We'll keep heading south until we reach a town with power, and then… I don't know, then we'll decide what to do next."

Garside nodded and sent the car rolling. "OK, south is good for me. I'm flying out of Los Angeles on Tuesday, so I was heading in that direction anyway."

Jack turned and stared in disbelief at Garside, searching for evidence that the man was just playing with him. Surely, he thought, this must be some kind of genius level trolling known only to the Brits. Surely nobody could be quite this clueless and still manage to get through the day without falling down, but no matter how hard he looked Jack could see no hint of guile in the man's expression. He felt a laugh bubble up from his deep in his gut, unwanted and unwelcome, but he couldn't hold it in.

"What's so funny?" Garside asked, perplexed, as

Jack began to laugh uncontrollably. He seemed alarmed by the tears streaming down Jack's face.

Jack struggled to take a breath. "You're flying out of LA?" he asked, trying to stifle a laugh that came more from stress and exhaustion than humor. "You might find that a little tricky, Doug. There's a good chance LA is a hole in the ground."

An amiable smile crept onto Garside's face as he shrugged. "Oh, it's not so bad," he said. "The traffic can be a bit of a nightmare, but at least the weather's pleasant."

It took a moment for Jack to understand Garside's error. He shook his head, wiping the tears from his eyes as he fought for breath. "No, not a *hole*. A hole in the *ground*. It was probably nuked. It's gone, just like everywhere else."

The smile began to slip from Garside's face, and he slowed the car to a crawl as he turned to stare at Jack, searching for the joke. "You're not serious?" he asked, the half smile still clinging on for dear life as doubt crept in.

"Of course I'm serious! Did you think a terrorist with one nuke on his hands would choose to launch it at Oregon? You think Eugene makes a good target? This thing is everywhere, Doug. They're attacking the entire west coast all the way from Seattle to LA. We're done. Up in God damned smoke. But what do you care, right? What did you say? You're just a visitor. It's not your place to comment."

Garside suddenly looked a decade older, small and hunched, his drawn expression like a death mask. Finally he spoke, his voice barely a whisper.

"My wife is in Los Angeles."

Jack felt as if all of the air had been suddenly sucked from the car. His manic, stressed laughter died away to silence, and his loathing of Garside was forgotten as a wave of sadness and loss emanated from the man.

"Oh, I'm so sorry," he muttered, unable to find anything better to say. Garside looked on the verge of tears. "Look, I don't know if it was really hit. Maybe I'm wrong. It probably *was* just Oregon," he lied, but it was clear from Garside's expression that he didn't believe him.

"She... she wanted to do a little shopping and spend some time on the beach," he mumbled, letting the car roll to a halt as if he'd lost all interest in moving forward. "She said she didn't want me getting in her hair."

His mouth opened and closed silently for a

moment. "I never enjoyed the beach. Never liked the feeling of sand between my toes, so Brenda told me to bugger off and spend a few days up in the woods where I'd be happy. You see, that's the thing about marriage," he said, gazing down at the gold band around his ring finger. "After a few years you stop trying to change each other. You just accept them for who they are and…" He trailed off. "She always loved the beach, but I didn't like the sand between my toes. Takes days to get rid of it."

Jack winced with discomfort, watching the man fall apart before his eyes. "Look, I'm sure she's fine. This was all over the news for hours before it happened. I'm sure they evacuated the cities in time. She's probably waiting for you right now, worried sick about where you are."

He looked over his shoulder at the rear seats, where Boomer was gnawing on one of his shoes. "Hey, why don't you get in the back and lay down for a while? You don't want to be driving while your mind's elsewhere. OK?"

Garside nodded. Without another word he pushed open the door and climbed out of the car, trudging to the back and climbing in without noticing that Boomer was still back there. His fear was forgotten now, and he didn't flinch as Boomer lay down beside him and rested her head in his lap, looking up at him with wide, sad eyes.

"Come on, Boomer, up front," Jack ordered as he climbed awkwardly into the driver's seat, but the dog paid no attention. When he settled behind the wheel he turned to find Garside nervously resting his hand on her back.

"It's OK," he mumbled, distractedly. "I think I'd like the company, if you don't mind." He sat bolt upright, still acting as if Boomer might attack at any moment, but it seemed as if there was some need strong enough to overcome his fear.

"Brenda always wanted a dog," he said, gently stroking Boomer's fur. "I never told her I was too afraid."

Jack remained silent. He couldn't think of anything to say, so he fixed his eyes on the dark road ahead, shifted into gear and drove.

•▼•

CHAPTER EIGHT
BACTINE WON'T CUT IT

KAREN STARED UP at the flickering flourescent light in the ceiling above her, waiting for the moment the room was plunged into darkness.

The generators had started to power down a little after nightfall, shutting down systems in some kind of power conserving sequence. The first to go were the cameras. Half the screens had gone dark, and then an hour later the rest had blinked out one after the other. The lights in the bathroom and break room had flickered out next, and then the hum of the refrigerator had fallen silent, quickly filling the room with the musty, plastic odor of melting freezer frost.

It was only when the strip lights in the office

began to flicker out one by one that Ramos finally spoke up.

"It's time," he said, staring fixedly at the clock on the wall.

Karen shook her head, pulling Emily's sleeping body closer towards her. "It's too soon, Doc. You said it yourself. You said we have to wait at least twenty four hours before leaving a safe shelter."

Ramos nodded. "I did say that, yeah, but this isn't a safe shelter anymore. It's only safe for me and Emily. Every moment you spend down here brings you a step closer to…" He didn't want to say it, but he didn't have to. "That makes it unsafe for all of us." He saw that Karen was about to protest, and he beat her to it.

"No more arguments. It's time."

Karen wanted to argue, but she knew he was right. Her condition had only grown worse since her exposure to the fallout. Her head was pounding behind her eyes, and her stomach stabbed at her with cramping pains. The skin around her neck was dry and cracked where the dust had gathered at her collar, and already the cracks looked inflamed.

Ramos had found a bottle of Bactine in a first aid kit in the break room while he searched for a bandage for the graze the bullet had scored into his arm, but she knew a dab of Bactine wouldn't cut it. Eventually one of her wounds would become infected, and then… then Emily would have to watch her mom die.

She looked down at her daughter, buried beneath one of the adult sized high visibility jackets they'd found in the lockers, and she reluctantly moved to wake her.

"Pumpkin?" She gently shook Emily by the shoulder. "Emily, wake up. It's time for us to go."

Emily moaned in her sleep, shrugging away her mom's hand. Karen knew she must be exhausted after the day she'd had. She'd already slept for hours, but it was clear she needed more. It was only when Karen reached under her arms and pulled her up that she began to stir.

"Come on, honey," she said, her voice soft. "Doctor Ramos says it's time to leave."

Emily frowned and rolled to her side, burying her head in Karen's lap.

"Come on, Emily," Ramos cajoled. "We have to go get that medicine to help your mom get better. What do you say?"

Emily finally began to move. Her eyes fluttered

open, but she didn't sit up.

"Mommy," she said, her voice a hoarse whisper. "Mommy, I don't feel so good." Her shoulders suddenly heaved, and without warning she leaned forward and vomited on the floor beside her.

Ramos was by her side in an instant. "It's OK, honey, just relax," he said, brushing back her hair and holding a hand against her forehead. He turned to Karen and whispered. "She's running a temperature."

"Mommy," Emily wept, gagging once again. "What's happening?"

"Don't worry, pumpkin, it's OK," Karen assured her, trying and failing to stay calm. She lowered her voice. "Doc, what's wrong with her?"

Ramos shook his head, lifting Emily up until she was sitting, propped against Karen's shoulder. "Emily, where does it hurt? Does your head hurt?"

Emily shook her head. "Nuh uh. Just my tummy, and…" she waved a hand around her throat. "It's itchy."

Karen tilted Emily's head back, pulling the collar of her jacket away from her neck, and when she saw what was beneath she recoiled in horror. "Doc!"

Ramos saw it. Running across the front of Emily's chest from one shoulder to the other was a line of radiation burns, bright pink and swollen. "Has this coat been outside?" he demanded, pulling it away from her inflamed skin.

"No! We got it out of the locker along with the rest of them. It's clean."

Ramos frowned, staring at the burns. "Then how…?" It finally dawned on him. "Oh, shit."

"What?" Karen demanded, panic creeping into her voice. "*What is it?*"

Ramos grabbed a bottle of water and began to douse the burns. "I should have figured it out sooner. I can't believe I didn't think about it, but I was distracted by you and my damned arm. Stupid."

"Doc, what is it? What are you talking about?"

Ramos emptied the water bottle and opened another. "Jared," he said. "It was Jared. He had his arm wrapped around Emily's throat."

Karen still wasn't getting it. "I… Are you saying he hurt her?"

Ramos nodded. "Not intentionally. He tracked it in with him. He was covered in the stuff, falling off him like dandruff."

"You mean…"

"Yeah." Ramos closed Emily's jacket back over the

swollen, angry burns. "I mean she has radiation poisoning, Karen." He swallowed, bracing himself for what was about to come. "And if she doesn't get treatment soon she'll die."

⁂

CHAPTER NINE
WELCOME TO PINE BLUFF

JACK BALANCED HIS cell phone on the steering wheel, glancing down at the screen whenever the unlit, snaking road ahead straightened out enough to allow it.

He wasn't expecting to find a signal. Hell, he hadn't seen so much as a working light bulb in hours, so he'd be amazed if his phone showed any bars, but in the distance he'd noticed something that gave him a glimmer of hope. It might just be his imagination and tired eyes playing tricks on him, but after hours of staring at a pitch black sky the darkness ahead seemed to be taking on a slightly different texture.

Directly above the car he could still see sharp pin

pricks of stars glimmering on a black velvet sky. It was the kind of night sky so clear that you could make out the curve of the Milky Way if you held still and let your eyes adjust. Up ahead, though, the crystal clear stars seemed to be turning muddy, fading into a black-orange haze above the endless forest.

Jack knew that sky well. It was the same sky he'd seen almost every night of his life above towns and cities, the glow of streetlights tempering nature's beauty, banishing all but the brightest of stars. On any other night he'd find the washed out haze an eyesore, but tonight… tonight it gave him hope.

He couldn't yet see the lights themselves, but he was certain that somewhere up ahead there was power. Somewhere nearby the lights were still shining, and in great enough numbers to cast their glow against the sky. After hours of walking and another couple of hours driving they were finally approaching the edge of the dead zone carved out by the EMP. Up ahead civilization began anew. Lights, heat, radio and TV, and – he crossed his fingers with hope – a cell signal.

He looked down again at the screen. Still no bars. "Come on," he whispered to himself. "Give me something, please."

"*Hmm?*" From the back seat came a yawn, and the slow groan of a waking stretch. "Did you say something?"

"Sorry, I didn't mean to wake you." Jack pointed out the windshield. "I think there are lights up ahead. We may be coming to a town."

Garside leaned forward between the seats, scanning the road ahead. "Oh, marvelous. Do you think they'll know what's happening?"

Jack shrugged. "Depends how bad it is, I guess. If they've got power the TV and radio may still be running. Maybe they're still picking up the news. Guess we'll have to wait and see."

"Fingers crossed."

Garside rested his chin on the back of the seat and gazed out the window, joining Jack in the hopeful search for light. He seemed deep in thought, lapsing into silence for a long spell, and Jack figured he was worried about what lay ahead. Worried about reaching the town and finding that the news was bad, that LA had been wiped from the map, and his wife with it. Jack was trying to think of some comforting words to offer when Garside finally cleared his throat.

"I could absolutely murder a cup of tea," he sighed. "I haven't had any all day."

Jack chuckled, baffled by Garside's priorities. "I think we have more important things to worry about than tracking down some Earl Grey, Doug."

Garside smiled and shook his head. "You may mock, Mr. Archer, but you just don't understand the relationship between an Englishman and his tea. You know the way you lot feel about your second amendment, thumping your chests and going on about your God given right to arm yourselves to the teeth?"

Jack nodded. "I guess so, if you want to put it like that."

"Well," Garside said, leaning back in his seat, "the English feel exactly the same way about a good cup of tea. You can pry my mug from my cold, dead hands."

Jack laughed. "OK, settle down, Heston. I'm sure we can find you something to drink, but first we're looking for a TV. Deal?"

Garside nodded. "Fair enough. I suppose I can deny myself for a few more minutes. I warn you, though, I can sometimes get a little tetchy when I go without my tea."

"You don't say," Jack muttered. "I never would have guessed." He turned his attention back to the road as Garside settled down in the back, driving on in silence, praying for the lights to appear each time the car rounded a bend in the road.

The exchange with Garside had perked him up a little, but he knew he couldn't go on like this much longer. He was beyond exhausted, running on fumes. His eyes felt like someone had gone to town on them with a belt sander, dry and scratchy from miles of driving without the aid of headlights. All he could think about was pulling over and resting them a while, but he was determined to keep going until he reached whatever lay ahead. He wouldn't be able to relax until he'd found the source of the lights.

Another twenty minutes passed before they finally appeared up ahead. As the car peaked a hill and began to weave down the other side a distant string of streetlights emerged from the forest, and Jack felt his foot press down on the gas. He pushed the car as hard as he dared along the dark, winding road, and after another few minutes of barreling around blind bends the lights finally appeared just a few dozen yards ahead. Jack eased off the gas, the tension drifting away as the car burst forth into their welcoming golden glow.

"Thank God for that," he sighed, squinting his eyes against the sudden brightness. "I thought we'd never see a streetlight again."

For another ten minutes the lights continued, a glowing ribbon cut through the darkness of the forest, before finally Jack spotted something in the distance other than the endless trees. It was a wooden sign, and a hundred yards beyond it was a small village, if it deserved even that diminutive title. It barely looked large enough to be marked on a map, just a handful of small stores and a few houses running along one side of the road. If it hadn't been for the streetlights Jack may have missed it entirely.

"Welcome to Pine Bluff," Garside read, peering out the window at the sign. He pushed up his glasses. "I must say, it doesn't look like they're rolling out the welcome mat."

Jack couldn't help but agree. The place looked completely dead. Half of the stores looked like they'd been closed long ago, and the rest seemed like they'd been abandoned in a hurry. Doors hung open and windows were broken. In front of each store Jack could see merchandise littering the sidewalks, as if the owners had packed in a rush by simply throwing everything they owned out through the doors and windows. In front of a convenience store a pallet of bottles had been dropped, and Jack pulled to the curb a few yards shy of a spray of glass shards glittering like diamonds across the asphalt.

"You wanna take a look around?" he asked, grabbing his phone and climbing out of the car.

Garside peered suspiciously out the window. "Are you sure it's safe out there?"

"Nope, not a clue." Jack held his phone above his head and craned his neck, as if a couple extra feet might make all the difference to the signal, but the screen still stubbornly refused to show him any bars. "Damn it," he muttered, slipping it into his pocket before looking back to Garside.

"Oh, come on, Doug. I'm sure it's perfectly safe. Looks like everybody left hours ago. Come on, Boomer, let's take a walk."

The dog perked up and leaped over the seats as Garside reluctantly pushed open the door, and she immediately ran towards the dropped pallet of bottles in front of the convenience store.

"Whoa, there," Jack warned, grabbing her by the collar and pulling back before she started lapping at broken glass. "Let's take a look at what we got here."

He crouched down at the side of the road, picking through the pallet until he found an intact bottle, and with a slap of his palm again the curb he popped the cap. "How do you feel about root beer, buddy?" he asked, pouring a splash into his palm for Boomer to lap up, and he laughed as she backed away as soon as she'd taken a taste, pawing at her muzzle with disgust.

"Yeah, I know, it's an acquired taste," he chuckled, throwing back the bottle for a gulp. "How about you, Doug? You want a root beer?"

Garside pursed his lips and shook his head. "*Yuck.* Far too sweet." He pointed towards the door of the convenience store. "I'm going to see if they have the makings of a cup of tea."

"Suit yourself," Jack said, pulling himself back to his feet with a tired groan. "Don't wander too far, though. I'm gonna go look for a TV or radio. Gimme a yell if you see one." He took another swig of root beer and began to wander along the street, peering in through store windows.

There didn't seem to be much to Pine Bluff. Beyond the handful of stores and what looked like a small white church at the far end of town the road quickly returned to dense forest. A narrow side road just before the stores ran to a small flat patch in the hilly terrain where a dozen or so wooden houses huddled close together, set back from the street. It seemed like one of those places you'd pass by on a road trip, and if you gave any thought to it at all it would be to wonder how the people who lived there could possibly earn a living way out in the middle of nowhere.

As he made his way down the road Jack noticed that even the stores looked out of place. The convenience store looked useful enough, but two doors down was a sporting goods store, and next door to that was a haberdashery, the sign above the door reading Pine Bluff Notions in curly, old fashioned script. Jack could almost understand the sporting goods store – maybe the forest around the town attracted weekend hikers – but how the hell could anyone make a living selling buttons and thread way out here in the woods? Who was traveling to Pine Bluff to buy thimbles?

"Small towns are weird, Boomer, am I right?" The dog looked up at him, panting happily as she trotted alongside. "Yeah, you know what I mean. You're a city dog, right? I bet you– "

Boomer broke into a run before Jack finished speaking, racing off ahead. "Oh sure, don't mind me," he called after her. "You'll tell me if I'm boring you, right?"

Boomer paid no attention. She trotted down the road, sniffing at the lamp posts and stoops, and she didn't stop until she reached the small parking lot beside the church. Jack limped after her, concerned that she might get her nose into something dangerous as she started snuffling through what looked like an abandoned bag of groceries dropped in the street at the edge of the lot. As he rounded the corner of the final store he saw that it wasn't the only one.

The parking lot looked like the aftermath of an explosion at a thrift store. A dozen or more rucksacks and suitcases littered the ground, some of them open, their contents blown in the breeze and trampled. An empty wheelchair was tipped onto its side, and beside it an A frame chalkboard had been knocked over and discarded. Jack made his way to it, kicking away an enormous floral dress that had caught itself on the frame.

Evacuation Point
One bag per person
No wheelchairs/strollers
Display photo ID before boarding
Departing 10PM

Jack stared at the board, and not for the first time he felt as if he was running just a few steps behind everyone else, playing catch up. All day, it seemed, people had been fleeing ahead of him, from the first people to grab the cabs at the airport to the first flights out of Renton, and now this. He was driving through a state that already felt hollowed out and emptied. The smart folks had left long ago. God only knew where they'd gone, but wherever it was–

Jack threw himself into an alert crouch as a sudden scream pierced the silence, and he turned in time to see Garside stumble backwards out of the convenience store and into the pool of light beneath a streetlight. He almost fell to the ground before recovering himself, running at full pelt towards Jack, a coffee mug clutched in a flailing hand and his jacket billowing out behind him like a tweed cape.

"*She has a gun!*" he cried, rounding the corner of the last store in the row and flattening himself against the side wall. "*Run!*"

•▼•

CHAPTER TEN
DID YOU SAY FRESNO?

JACK FELT HIS heart leap to his throat as he scanned around for cover, cursing when he saw that the only things within diving distance were the tipped over wheelchair and the abandoned chalkboard. The church was a good twenty yards away, and the cover of the trees further still. He was completely exposed and helpless. If someone came out shooting there was nothing he could do to stop them, and nowhere to hide. He stood rooted to the spot, frozen by terror.

"Hello?" A woman's voice called out from the convenience store. "Can I help you?"

Jack barely heard the voice above the thumping of

his heart, but when it filtered past his fear he felt confusion overwhelm his fear. That certainly didn't sound like someone about to launch an armed assault. It sounded like a friendly young woman greeting a customer in a store.

"Hello?" he called back hesitantly. Even as he spoke he felt stupid, standing out in the open. "Hey… umm, are you planning to shoot?"

The woman appeared around from the door of the convenience store and began to approach at a sauntering pace. "Sorry, I'm not sure I heard you right. Say that again?"

Jack coughed awkwardly. "Umm… I said, are you planning to shoot?" He could feel himself beginning to burn with embarrassment at such a stupid question.

The young woman reached the corner of the final store, and as she stepped onto the parking lot she jumped with fright at the sight of Garside pressed flat against the wall right beside her.

"Jeez, you scared the life out of me! What are you doing hiding like that?" She turned to Jack. "And why on earth would I be planning to shoot?"

Jack felt his knotted muscles relax as his body stood down from red alert. The woman looked to be around her early twenties, dressed casually in jeans and a plaid shirt, and at her hip a pistol remained firmly clipped in its holster. Boomer padded over to her cheerfully, leaning into her hand as she scratched her behind her ears. "Hey, cutie, how's it going?" she said, dropping to her haunches to play with the dog.

"Sorry about that," Jack said, a slight smile playing on his lips. "My friend here's a Brit. I don't think he's accustomed to seeing people wearing holsters."

Garside slowly relaxed, trying to reclaim what dignity he could by pretending he'd been casually leaning against the wall, not trying to press himself through it. "I was just a little alarmed," he claimed. "Where I come from we don't go around shooting each other."

The woman let out a laugh. "We don't go around shooting each other here, either," she said. "You're in Oregon, not the Wild West." She turned back to Jack and gave him a conspiratorial wink. "So, what brings you guys to Pine Bluff?"

"Just passing through on our way south, ma'am," Jack said, taking a swig from his root beer before something occurred to him. "Sorry, do you own the convenience store? I thought everyone had left town. I can pay for the drink."

She shook her head. "No, you can help yourself. Mine's the sporting goods store. Well, it's not *mine*. I just work there. I'm Cathy."

"Jack. And this is Doug."

Garside nodded curtly. "Douglas," he corrected. "Douglas Garside. How do you do? Apologies for the histrionics."

Cathy waved his apology away. "Don't worry about it. I guess everyone's a little on edge today."

Jack took a seat on the curb beside Boomer as she enjoyed the attention from Cathy. "Are you on your own?" he asked, before it occurred to him that the question might seem a little threatening coming from a strange man. "I mean, how come you didn't leave town with everyone else?" He nodded towards the chalkboard with the scrawled instructions. "There was an evacuation from here, right?"

Cathy nodded. "Oh yeah, they came through here. A bunch of soldiers showed up in a school bus and told us they were taking us to some refugee camp over in Namath Falls. That's about an hour or two east of here, so I guess they figured it'd be safe enough."

"But you didn't get on the bus?"

Cathy shook her head. "Nuh uh. They said there

wasn't enough room for all of us, so they pulled a bunch of us out of line and told us there'd be a second bus along a little later."

"The second bus didn't show up?"

Cathy shook her head and gave him a wry smile. "There never *was* a second bus. They were lying to us."

"Wait, what?" Jack couldn't believe what he was hearing. "You're saying they intentionally abandoned you? You can't be serious."

"Believe it," Cathy insisted. "I didn't figure out what was going on until the bus was rolling out of town, and by then it was too late to do anything about it. I guess they thought this was the best way to avoid a confrontation."

"What did you figure out? What am I missing?"

Cathy rolled back the sleeve of her shirt, revealing a row of track marks running from her elbow halfway to her wrist. "There were six of us pulled out of line, and it finally clicked when I realized I'd seen them all in Doctor Keeler's waiting room down at Medford. We were pretty much the only sick people in town. Quite a coincidink, right?"

Garside pursed his lips with distaste, staring at the trail of injection marks. "You're a drug addict?"

"What? Oh God, no!" Cathy laughed. "I've never even smoke a joint. I just have a condition that has to be treated with intravenous injections."

Jack frowned, puzzled. "Wait, are you saying they left you behind because…"

His voice trailed off. Finally it began to make sense.

Of course they left the sick behind. Condition Black would be useless if it was only applied to the hospitals. The idea behind it was to get rid of *everyone* who might spread illness through a refugee camp, not just the folks laid up in hospital beds. The army must have been screening evacuees as they boarded buses and passed through checkpoints, trying to weed out the sick before they could reach the camps. There was just one thing Jack couldn't figure out.

"How did they know you were sick?"

Cathy rolled her sleeve back down her arm. "Doctor Keeler was with the soldiers. He's the local doc down in Medford. Pretty much everyone around here goes to him, so I guess he must have handed over a list of his patients. I don't suppose doctor/patient confidentiality counts for much when there's a guy with a rifle asking the questions."

"Yeah, I guess it wouldn't," Jack agreed, nodding sympathetically.

He was just blown away by the level of organization that must have gone into the evacuation. Condition Black must have been much better planned than he'd assumed, if the government had the ability to track down individual doctors on a moment's notice. Maybe they even had access to prescription records and insurance forms, all the data they'd need to identify those who might put a population at risk. "So who was– "

"What's wrong with you?" Garside butted in, and then immediately blushed as he realized how rude he was being. "Sorry, forget I asked. It's none of my business, I'm sure."

Cathy waved away his apology with a smile. "Don't worry about it, it's nothing embarrassing. I've got Wilson's Disease. It's a genetic thing. My body can't get rid of copper fast enough, so it builds up in my organs and causes all kinds of problems."

"Wilson's? You take penicillamine for that?" Jack asked.

Cathy nodded. "Uh huh. And daily Cyclosporine injections."

Jack raised his eyebrows. "Anti-rejection meds? You

had a transplant?"

"Yeah, my liver, three years ago," she replied, surprised. "What are you, a doctor or something?"

Jack nodded. "Used to be, yeah. How are you set for meds?"

"Not too bad," Cathy shrugged. "I've got enough Cyclo to last a couple of months, but I'm running a little short of the penicillamine. Maybe two weeks before I hit trouble, if I can't find any more. Why?"

"Nothing. It's just… well, that's why they didn't take you. You'd be a burden."

As soon as he said it he wanted to swallow the words. "Sorry, I didn't mean that to sound so blunt. I just mean those are pretty specialized meds you're using. They won't have them wherever they're evacuating people. I'm guessing the other folks who got left behind all needed regular medication too, right?"

Cathy nodded. "I guess so. I know Mr. Reeves has diabetes, and Sally Becker has some kind of blood pressure thing. They probably all needed something."

"And where are they now?"

She shrugged and pointed vaguely towards the east. "Mr. Reeves has an old Winnebago. He said if the government wouldn't let him go along he'd just head inland and find someplace to wait it out until he can come home. Everyone went with him."

"How come you didn't join them?" Jack asked. "Seems like that would have been the safest option."

Cathy chuckled and shook her head. "If you ever met Mr. Reeves you wouldn't ask that question. If I had to spend a week in his Winnebago playing I Spy and fighting off his offers of back rubs I think I'd eat a bullet." She reached out and took the bottle of root beer from Jack, taking a swig before handing it back. "I'm OK. I figured… well, this is Pine Bluff. Nobody's nuking Pine Bluff, right? As long as the power stays on I figure it's safe to stay."

Jack felt his heart pick up speed at the mention of the power. He got the feeling that a moment he'd been dreading was about to arrive.

"Is your TV still working?" he asked. "Or the radio? Do you know what's going on out there? Do they know who attacked us?"

Cathy shook her head. "We never get a good signal out here so I don't bother with the radio, but the TV stopped broadcasting maybe four or five hours ago. The set still works just fine, but maybe a transmitter got knocked out or something because all I can pick up is static."

Right away Jack knew what had happened. "It was the EMP." He saw Cathy's confused expression. "An electromagnetic pulse," he explained. "There was a nuclear blast maybe sixty miles north of here just before nightfall. It knocked out the power for miles. This is the first place we've seen where the lights are still on, but I've heard that an EMP can screw up the atmosphere for hours. It could be blocking the satellite downlink for the TV."

Cathy looked alarmed. "Sixty miles from here? You're *kidding!* What about fallout? Are we gonna get sick?"

"Don't worry," Jack assured her. "It was a high altitude blast. I don't know much about this kind of thing, but I know that you only get fallout from explosions at ground level. It's all the dirt that gets thrown up in the atmosphere. You don't get any of that when the blast is in the upper atmosphere. Not much radiation at all. All it really does is screw up the power."

Garside politely cleared his throat to attract Cathy's attention. "Before the TV stopped working, miss, what did you hear? Was there any news about Los Angeles?"

"And what about San Francisco?" Jack added.

"And Modesto?"

Cathy pulled Boomer close, hugging her like a comfort blanket. She seemed reluctant to speak. "Why?" she eventually asked. "Do you know people there?"

Jack nodded. "Doug's wife is in LA, and I'm heading down to meet my wife and daughter in Modesto."

Cathy didn't speak for a long time, but Jack already knew what was coming. His heart hardened as he saw Cathy's eyes glisten with tears, and her cheeks flushed red.

"I'm so sorry," she said, each softly spoken word hitting Jack like a fist. "They're gone."

Jack slumped forward, his head falling into his hands as the news hit him. He felt like she'd just torn the soul from his body.

He'd expected San Francisco to be hit. It was a major city and an obvious target, and he'd been prepared for the news as much as anyone could be, but deep down he'd believed that Modesto would be a safe haven. It was a city of barely two hundred thousand, an anonymous inland sprawl few outside California ever thought about. It didn't seem to have any strategic value. It only just scraped into the top twenty largest cities in the state. Why would anyone bother to attack it? It just didn't make any sense.

Running on numb autopilot he found himself pulling his phone from his pocket. He brought up his messages and blankly stared at the words on the screen. The last words his wife would ever have for him.

Where are you? Pls tell me you left Seattle. News says it could be hit by nuke. Me+Em+Doc headed to Anne's place. Pls call when you can.

Love you.

He tried to stop himself from thinking about it, but he couldn't stop the tears from pricking at his eyes as he wondered where they'd been when they died. Had they been caught in San Francisco, fighting through the crowds as they tried to evacuate? Had they made it to Anne's farm? Did they think they were safe when the flash arrived on the horizon? Had it hurt? Had Emily been scared? Had she been with her mom when the time came?

Jack didn't even notice the tears streaming down his cheeks until Cathy put her arm over his shoulder, pulling him in for a hug while Boomer sat between them.

"I'm so sorry," she said. "For both of you. But

look, you shouldn't give up. Doug, I heard there was a massive effort to evacuate LA. It was going on for hours before it was hit. They *must* have gotten most of the people out. And Jack, the same goes for San Francisco. And the news said that the one that hit Fresno landed near the airport. That's about five miles from downtown. I'm sure plenty of people survived."

Jack was only half listening, wallowing in grief, but her words found their way through. "Wait, did you say Fresno?"

"Yeah. Apparently it went off course and overshot the city. Maybe there was– "

"I didn't ask about Fresno," Jack interrupted, his heart suddenly racing. "I asked about Modesto."

Cathy took a sharp breath and covered her mouth with a hand. "Oh my God, I'm so sorry, I must have misheard you!" She frowned, trying to remember the news reports. "I… I'm not certain, but I don't remember hearing anything about Modesto. They definitely got San Francisco and Sacramento, then Fresno and Bakersfield were a few minutes later. It all happened so quickly, and the news was so crazy, it was just… Everyone was yelling. Nobody knew what was going on, but Modesto? I just don't remember hearing anyone mention it."

Jack looked down at his phone once more, staring at the final words of the message.

Love you

"They're alive," he said, finally. He didn't know how he knew, but he could just feel it in his bones. Karen was a survivor. She was smart and tough, tougher than Jack could ever be. If there was even the slightest chance to escape he knew she'd have grabbed hold of it with both hands.

"They're alive, and I'm going to find them." He turned to Garside, slouched against the wall, his head in his hands. "That goes for your wife too, Doug. You're going to find Brenda. Now's not the time to give up hope. We're going south."

He pushed himself from the curb, his energy suddenly renewed, and as he began to walk back to the car he felt Cathy's hand grab his sleeve.

"Hey, I don't want to sit this out up here on my own. Do you think I can come with?"

Jack reached down and took her hand, pulling her to her feet. "The more the merrier," he said, sealing it with a shake.

He turned to Garside. "Doug? Get in the car. Let's go find our families."

Cathy looked back down the street at the Civic. "You're driving *that*? No, no, no, if we're heading into this mess we're not taking a little Japanese toy car."

Garside scowled. "That's my rental, of course we're taking it. I don't want to lose my deposit."

Cathy shook her head. "It's no good. And besides, I think we're way past worrying about money. We'll take my truck." She reached into the pocket of her jeans, pulled out a keychain and tossed it in the air, the streetlights catching the Ford logo before she caught it. She flashed Garside a grin.

"Welcome to America, Doug."

•▼•

CHAPTER ELEVEN
A THOUSAND LITTLE STEPS

KAREN HAD NO more tears to spare.

No more breath to spare, either. She leaned against the closest car, struggling to stay on her feet as the world swam around her. Her legs trembled with the strain after just a few dozens steps, and she dreaded to think how she'd feel by the time they finally reached the mainland two miles to the east. The bridge seemed to stretch out ahead of her for an eternity, an endless traffic-cluttered ribbon.

It wasn't the radiation sickness that was holding her back – at least she didn't think it was. It was just exhaustion and hunger, a gaping hole in her stomach that hadn't been filled in… what, a day and a half?

Damn, she thought, counting off the hours since she'd last taken a bite. *It's no wonder I'm shaky.* More than thirty hours had passed since her last meal, and even that had been nothing heavier than a sandwich and a couple of dry crackers, a hurried snack while she did the laundry.

"How are you feeling?" Ramos stopped and called back, his voice full of concern. He could see just how weak she was. "Do you need to take a break?"

Karen shook her head and waved him on. She knew Ramos was only being polite. They couldn't afford to rest here in the fallout zone, even twelve hours after the attack. It would still kill them if they gave it the chance.

"Go on ahead," she said, pushing herself away from the car and forcing herself onward. "I'll catch up. Just get Emily out of here."

Ramos nodded uncertainly, watching her take a few shaky steps forward, but eventually he moved on, powering ahead with a strength Karen only wished she could muster.

Ramos knew Emily was the priority. He'd wrapped her as tightly as he could in the high visibility jacket, trying to seal her off in a self contained bubble protected from the fallout, but he knew it was far from perfect. Even if her cocoon was completely airtight she'd still be absorbing radiation out here. She'd already received a dose higher than her small body could shake off, and every moment out on this bridge would only push her closer to the edge.

They walked on, Karen falling back two steps for every ten Ramos took, and by the time they crossed the halfway point of the bridge she was already a hundred yards behind him and wheezing for air. Ramos turned and watched her struggle onward, but still he didn't stop and wait. He knew that if he turned back to help her she'd use her last breath to curse him.

Karen was feeling the cold now. The clammy air cut through her own jacket, but unlike Emily she wasn't wrapped up tight, protected from the elements. There had been no spare trousers left in the lockers. The one pair she'd found had already been contaminated during her walk to shut down the fans, so the knee length jacket was all she had to keep out the chill. She limped along with her bare legs ending in a pair of men's boots even larger than the last pair she'd worn. It seemed the people who worked in the tunnel all had clown feet.

The cold didn't really bother her, though. If

anything it invigorated her, and drove her on. The cold bite told her that she was still alive, and her stinging skin reminded her that at the end of this, somewhere God knows how far along the road, there would be a hot bath waiting for her. She could lay back and let the warmth envelop her, and when it finally drained away it would take with it every last trace of the ash, dust and dirt that tainted her skin. It was concern for her daughter that was keeping her on her feet, but she couldn't deny that the wish for a bath was helping her pace.

She fought her aching legs and increased her speed, fixing her eyes on the mainland far ahead. There were still lights on out there. It seemed unbelievable, but just a few miles east of a nuclear blast the power was somehow still running. The streetlights still burned. Houses were intact, warm and cozy, just as they had been yesterday, and the shore was lit up like a string of Christmas lights. Oakland had never looked so beautiful.

For twenty minutes Karen forced herself to clear her mind. She refused to think of anything but putting one foot in front of the other, slow and steady, counting her shuffling, halting steps until she finally reached one thousand, and then she stopped, took a short break to rest her throbbing feet, and began counting once again.

She'd reached one thousand three times over by the time the bridge reached the mainland, and she'd counted out another seven hundred when she finally found Ramos waiting for her amid a mass of vehicles packed closely together, blocking the road. Emily had vomited down his shoulder, but he didn't seem to care.

"Looks like this is why the bridge got backed up," he said. At the head of the tangled mass a school bus was stopped side on, straddling three lanes with one of its tires blown out. The road itself was six lanes wide, but the other three lanes were blocked by two dozen cars that had tried all at the same time to squeeze through a gap only large enough for three, four at a push. When the bus stopped it had probably only taken a few minutes for the rest of the road to jam up.

"So stupid," Ramos sighed, resting against the side of the bus. "Why didn't they just push this thing out of the way? They could have cleared the road in a couple of minutes."

Karen shrugged. "Panic, I guess. People don't think clearly when they're scared." She looked back at the bridge, at the line of cars running all the way back to the island. "It only takes one driver to lose his cool and abandon his car, and then..." she swept her hand along the length of the bridge. "There must have been thousands of people stuck out here when the fallout started."

She pointed at a silver Prius that had wedged an old Buick up against the central divider, blocking the highway down to a single lane. "I wonder how many people this jackass killed because he couldn't drive in a straight line."

The road ahead of the Prius was clear. Karen moved to the driver's side of the car and saw that the bodywork had become caught up in the Buick's wheel arch, but a firm kick was enough to free it. The driver could have done that in just a few seconds. Hell, he could have just thrown the car into reverse and pulled himself loose, but instead it looked like he'd panicked and run. His mistake had blocked two of the three remaining lanes, and sentenced everyone behind him to death.

Karen sighed and peered in through the window. "Oh well, it's ours now. The keys are still in the ignition." A thought occurred to her as she reached out to grab the door handle. "Wait, is this safe? I mean, are the cars radioactive?"

Ramos walked to the back and pulled open the door, lowering Emily onto the back seat with a grunt of effort. "Radioactive? Well, yeah. *Everything* out here is radioactive, but we've reached the point where we don't have the luxury of avoiding it. That ship sailed a while back. Now we're just making choices that limit our exposure as much as possible. It could be a hundred miles to the safe zone, and if we try to walk it we'll have gills by the time we get there." He let out a chuckle, but it was clear he was forcing it. They both knew the truth. If they tried to walk all three of them would be dead by sunrise.

Karen pulled her sleeve over her hand to pull the handle, shivering with disgust as she noticed the dust falling from the door. "I just feel… urgh, I don't want to touch anything."

"That's good," Ramos reassured her. "It means you're thinking straight. You won't make any dumb mistakes. But our best chance of survival is just to get through this as quickly as possible, so don't worry too much about– hey, what do you think you're doing?"

Karen shot him a confused look. "What do you mean? Nothing. I'm getting in the car."

"Not in the driver's seat, you're not." Ramos

gestured to the rear door. "I know you like to be behind the wheel, but you're not driving in your condition."

"My condition? Doc, I feel OK, seriously. I'll be fine."

Ramos took her by the shoulder and gently but firmly guided her to the back of the car. "You're not fine, you just *think* you're fine. Radiation sickness can be unpredictable. You can feel on top of the world one minute and coughing up blood the next, and I'd just as soon not be doing eighty down the highway when your body decides it's time to pass out."

Karen protested. "Do you even know how to drive?"

"Of course. Just because I don't own a car doesn't mean I never learned. I was driving while you still had pink tassels hanging from your bike. Now get in and take care of your daughter. No arguments."

Karen finally relented, lowering herself on aching legs to the rear seat beside Emily. She didn't even know why she'd tried to resist. She *wanted* to be in the back with her daughter. She didn't want to spend a second away from her while she was sick. And besides, she was about ten miles beyond exhausted. Her legs throbbed with the strain of walking the bridge. What she needed more than anything was a meal and a sleep. She liked to be in control, but she couldn't deny she was happy to see Ramos climb into the driver's seat.

She looked down to find that Emily was sleeping. Unconscious, in any case, but she didn't seem to be in much discomfort. Her face was pale and there was a little vomit crusted in her hair, but she didn't seem to be suffering. Karen gently lifted her daughter's head from the seat and slid beneath her, resting the little girl in her lap. Emily shifted in her sleep and let out a mutter.

"You ready to go?" Ramos whispered, trying not to wake Emily, and when Karen gave a nod he switched the air to recirculate and slapped closed the air vents, then turned the key.

Nothing happened. There was no sound. For a moment Karen thought the car was a dud, but then she heard a soft beep from the dash, warning Ramos that he wasn't wearing his seatbelt. It was only when they began to creep forward that Karen remembered it was a Prius. It was running on its batteries.

As Ramos picked up speed on the empty highway Karen scanned around the back of the car, searching for anything that might be useful. What she *really* wanted were some warm clothes, but instead her eye caught something else. Down in the passenger footwell on the other side of the car she noticed a brown paper grocery bag, and – careful not to disturb Emily – she stretched over to grab it with the tips of her fingers. "Hang on, we got something here." She made a final lunge to reach it, pinching the paper between her fingers and dragging it close enough to lift. "Jackpot. Looks like the driver packed himself a lunch."

Ramos smiled. "Perfect. I'm so hungry I could eat my own arm. What do we have?"

"Looks like candy and soft drinks, mostly. I get the feeling the owner of this car wasn't a member of a gym." Karen dug through the bag with undisguised excitement, and then a thought struck her. "Hey, is this stuff safe?"

"Depends what you mean by safe," Ramos replied with a chuckle, and then he caught Karen's *I'm in no mood* expression in the rear view.

"Don't worry. Anything in a wrapper should be fine, but I'd steer clear of fruit with edible skin. It's only the fallout itself that's radioactive. It can't pass that radioactivity onto anything it touches, so the only risk is in eating the fallout itself."

Karen set aside a six pack of sugary soft drinks, a baggie of bland trail mix and an apple, and then she saw them, hidden at the bottom of the bag behind a bundle of tissues, and her heart skipped a beat. For a moment all the terrible things that had happened over the last twenty four hours faded from memory. Everything was right with the world, and all the horror seemed inconsequential compared to what was sitting there waiting for her, calling out to her.

It was a half dozen Twinkies.

"Oh my God," she gushed, tearing the wrapper from the first and stuffing it whole into her mouth. She spoke again, her voice muffled, spraying crumbs from her lips. "I haven't let myself eat one of these in about ten years."

She reclined in the seat, eyes blissfully closed, chewing on the mass of sweet creamy sponge even as she unwrapped the second. "Oh, Twinkies, how I missed you." It was just as delicious and terrible as she'd remembered, and exactly what she was craving.

"Umm, you might want to go easy on those things," Ramos warned, watching in the rear view as Karen took another bite. "Pace yourself."

"Are you my personal trainer now?" she laughed, the sugar already lifting her spirits. "Today isn't the day to worry about my waistline, Doc."

"No, it's not that. It's just we tell patients to stick to bland foods for a few days after radiation therapy. In your condition your stomach will be pretty delicate, and it might reject anything with too much…" His voice trailed off as he caught sight of her in the rear view. "Yeah, there it is."

Karen had stopped chewing. Half a Twinkie sat tucked in her cheeks as she took slow, deep breaths, fighting off a wave of nausea. The color drained from her face.

"Doc, I think I'm gonna– "

She slapped at the power window controls, and with a sudden lurch she bounced Emily's head from her lap and made it to the window just in time to lean out and vomit down the side of the car.

"*Yeeeeeaaaah*," Ramos drawled, trying to block out the sound of Karen's retching. "I tried to warn you. Radiation sickness and Twinkies don't really go together."

•⁊•

CHAPTER TWELVE
AS TALL AS HE'D EVER BE

JACK DREAMED ABOUT the end of the world.

He was standing in the living room of his poky apartment in Excelsior, looking out through the dusty bay window on a dark and overcast San Francisco. The clouds above the city were a deep blue and black, a bruised sky that threatened to burst at any moment, and as he watched it he felt a strange sense of foreboding.

He didn't know how, but he could sense that something was wrong with the familiar view. Something terrible was about to happen out there, and there was nothing he could do to stop it. All he could do was watch, powerless and impotent, trapped behind the glass, a bystander as events unfolded, and it wasn't long before the danger made itself known. He felt his eye drawn to an enormous angry storm cloud looming over downtown, and as he watched he saw something punch through, black and ominous, falling swiftly toward the city below.

Even at this distance Jack knew what it was long before it hit the ground. He knew what was about to happen, but no matter how hard he slammed his fists on the window the people walking outside didn't seem to hear him. They wouldn't look his way. He couldn't warn them. All he could do was stare at the missile as it plummeted silently toward the ground.

He looked back down at the street, and his heart began to pound as he saw them. Karen and Emily were walking hand in hand along the sidewalk beneath his window. They were smiling, swinging their arms, chatting without a care in the world, and behind them the missile continued to fall. Jack pounded on the glass with his fists until it felt like his bones were breaking, but he didn't even make a sound. Even when he screamed at the top of his voice there was only silence.

He turned back to his tiny, messy living room, desperately searching for something, *anything* he could use to break the window. He tossed aside papers and flipped tables on end, and finally he settled on the heavy wooden rocking chair that used to sit out on the porch at the old house, back when they'd been a family. The chair was so heavy he could barely lift it, an antique given to Karen by her father, carved from thick mahogany. He grunted with effort as he hefted it over his shoulder, and with all his strength he swung it at the window.

The chair shattered into a million pieces of kindling with the first blow. A shock of pain radiated up Jack's arms from the impact, but the glass didn't even tremble, didn't even scratch. It was as if he were trying to break through a solid steel wall.

Jack dropped the splintered remains of the chair and went back to beating his fists against the glass, screaming silently in the vacuum until it felt as if his vocal cords would spring from his throat. His fists bled, and he barely noticed the tears of frustration streaming down his face.

Now someone else appeared beside Emily, and suddenly... suddenly he'd *always* been there, walking alongside them. Jack pressed himself against the window, tears streaming down his face as he longed with every fiber of his being to be down there with them.

It was Robbie, standing in his pajamas, a wide smile on his face and eyes gleaming with excitement. He stood a foot shorter than his little sister in his socked feet, as tall as he'd ever be, his beaming face hidden beneath a thick mop of brown hair that swallowed combs, that always seemed as if it was being tousled by an unseen hand.

Robbie raised his arms to Karen, squeezing his hands into tiny fists, begging to be picked up and spun around, and he shrieked with delight when his mom obliged. From two floors up Jack could hear his laughter. It was all he could hear, even when his own cries were silenced.

"*Airplane!*" Robbie squealed, his voice cracking with delight as his legs swung out behind him.

And then Emily finally saw him. She tugged at her mom's skirt and pointed up at the window.

"Mommy, it's Daddy!" she yelled, smiling up at him. "*Hi, Daddy!*"

Karen looked up and noticed Jack pounding on the glass, and now all three of them waved happily, smiling at him, oblivious to the danger. Oblivious to his terror.

And then the missile reached the ground.

There was a flash, brighter than anything he'd ever seen. The world vanished in the glare, blinding Jack for a long moment, and as the mushroom cloud blossomed above the city Karen and the kids just stood and watched, pointing and staring in wonder as if they were watching a fireworks display. They watched as the buildings exploded into matchwood and the roads were torn from the ground in strips. They watched as cars and trucks were tossed into the air like toys, as the air itself ignited and began to burn with an unimaginable heat. They were still smiling. Still happy, right up to the moment the shock wave reached them.

"*Jack!*"

He opened his eyes with a start, his heart thumping in his chest and his hands clenched into fists. A sheen of sweat had left his shirt clinging to his skin.

He looked around the car, wide eyed and with no idea were he was. Out the window there was only darkness, and then a brief flash of white passed through the car as they sped by a streetlight. Jack turned away from the window, blinking and confused, and it finally began to come back to him.

He was in the truck. He'd handed Garside the

wheel and gone for a nap in the back beside… he fumbled for her name for a moment in his half-awake fug of confusion. Young girl. A little quirky. Carried a gun...

Cathy! He'd gone to sleep beside Cathy.

She looked over at him with a raised eyebrow. "I think you were having a bad dream. You OK?" she asked with concern. "You were yelling pretty loud."

Jack rubbed his eyes with his knuckles, stifling a yawn as he pulled himself up in his seat. "Yeah, I'm fine. Sorry, I do that sometimes. I know it's a little weird."

Cathy chuckled and shook her head. "If you think that's weird then you don't know weird. When I was a kid my grandma lived with us, and she used to sleepwalk into my room in the middle of the night."

"Well, that's not so strange," Jack replied, trying to distract himself from the memory of the nightmare. When he closed his eyes all he could see was Robbie's smiling face, just as the shock wave hit. "I think a lot of people sleepwalk every so often. My brother used to do it all the time when we were young."

"Yeah, I guess so," Cathy agreed, "but most people don't sleepwalk into your bedroom and take a leak in your toy chest."

Jack gave her a double take, checking for a hint that she might be joking. "She peed in your– ?"

Cathy held up her fingers. "Five times. Five times I got that little midnight surprise before my dad finally let me put a lock on my door." She laughed at the memory. "There's nothing worse than waking up to find a confused old lady peeing over your soft toys with her lacy nightdress bundled around her waist."

Jack grinned. "Oh, I don't know. I can think of at least one thing worse than that."

"Oh you think so, do you?" she asked, doubtfully. "What could possibly be worse that your grandma peeing all over your favorite toys?"

Jack stretched, letting her wait for a few beats before replying. "Just be thankful she was only going number one."

Cathy snorted with disgusted laughter. "Oh, *gross!*" She leaned over the headrest to the front seat. "Doug, did you hear that? Jack just said that– "

Garside sighed. "Yes, yes, toilet humor. It's all extremely hilarious to Americans, I'm sure. Maybe for an encore you can regale each other with a chorus of flatulence, or perhaps burp the alphabet."

Cathy sat back and smirked, pushing up the tip of her nose with a finger. "Sir Douglas is not amused,

Mr. Archer. From now on we must refrain from all mention of bodily functions lest we offend his highness."

"Lighten up, Doug," Jack chided. "There's nothing wrong with a little laughter to relieve the tension." He turned to Cathy and winked. "In fact, I feel a little tension building up right now. It's… oh, wait for it, here it comes." He tucked in his chin, opened his mouth and let out a long burp into Garside's ear.

Cathy burst out laughing, and Jack leaned back in his seat with a satisfied grin. "If you want me to do the entire alphabet you'll have to pull over and get me a Coke."

Garside narrowed his eyes in the rear view. "How you people ever became a superpower is quite beyond me. I'm not sure how you found the time to build the world's largest economy *and* perfect this comic mastery."

"We multitask, Doug," Jack laughed, leaning over the seat in front. In the front passenger seat Boomer was coiled up, her legs twitching as she dreamed. Garside had his hand at the scruff of her neck, gently scratching the folds of fat behind her collar.

"Not afraid any more?"

Garside looked down at the dog, almost surprised

to notice his own hand. He quickly snatched it away, and for a moment it looked as if he might say something cutting, but then he returned to Boomer's collar and gave her another scratch. "Well, I… I suppose I'm warming to the idea of dogs," he said. "This one, at least, doesn't appear to be a slavering beast intent on murder."

"No, she's a big softy," Jack smiled and patted him on the shoulder. "I'm sure Brenda will be pleased to hear you're getting over your fear. Maybe you guys can finally get a dog of your own when you get home."

"You never know," Garside replied. "Though that all depends if we even get to her. I'd be amazed if this thing makes it all the way without us having to stop and drill an oil well." He tapped the dash. "In England we have this incredible new thing called fuel economy. Maybe you're not familiar with it, because apparently your carmakers aren't. This silly penis extension seems to get about ten miles to the gallon."

Jack leaned over the seat, sucking air through his teeth when he saw the needle hovering just above the red line.

"Ouch. You can blame that on good old fashioned American muscle, Doug. Enough torque to kick start a dying star, but as thirsty as a drunk uncle at a wedding. Have we passed any gas stations recently?"

Garside shook his head. "Not since we left the highway, no."

"OK, we should keep our eyes open." He looked out the window, and for the first time noticed that they were on a narrow, single lane road. "Wait, how come we're not on the highway? How long was I out?"

"Just an hour or so. As for why we're not on the highway you should ask your partner in comedic crime back there," Garside said. "She's giving the directions. I'm just the chauffeur."

"We had to get off, genius," Cathy insisted. "If we'd stayed on the 5 we'd have ended up driving right through downtown Sacramento, and unless you've got a few radiation suits hidden in your pocket it's probably not a great idea to head in that direction. And besides, this might be my first apocalypse but I've seen enough movies to know that everyone heads for the highway when the shit hits the fan. It was only a matter of time before we hit a hundred mile tailback or, y'know, some kinda weird Max Max raiders who want to kill us for our guzzleine."

Jack sat back with a shrug. "OK, apart from the

Mad Max thing I take your point, but where the heck are we? This barely even looks like a road."

Cathy reached into the net pocket in the back of the driver's seat and pulled out a folding California road map. She unfolded a half dozen panels, spread the map out on her lap and flipped on the overhead light. "We're here. No, wait…" She traced her finger along a road that looked just like a hundred others. "Sorry, here. I think. More or less."

Jack raised an eyebrow. "More or less?"

Cathy shrugged. "That's as good as you'll get out of me. I can read orienteering maps, but when it comes to roads I've been ruined by Google just like everyone else. I'm used to seeing a little blue dot that tells me where I am."

Jack pulled the map from her lap and found the road she was pointing at. "So we're on Route 36?"

"Yeah, I'm 99% sure," she nodded. "Though I haven't seen any signs in a while. Pretty soon we should reach Lake Almanor and take a right onto the 89, then after a while that leads to the 70. After about four fingers that turns back into the– "

"I'm sorry. Four fingers?"

"Yeah, four fingers." She laid her hand palm down across the map. "See? One, two, three, four."

"You know there's a distance scale in the corner of the map, right?"

Cathy waved his suggestion away. "Anyway, after however many miles is four fingers the road turns back into the 89 for some reason, then we follow it all the way down to Lake Tahoe. After that there are a bunch of other roads, but I haven't worked that part out yet. Should be simple enough."

Jack gave her a bemused smile. "Well, I don't know about you, but I'm just brimming with confidence." He peered at the map, trying to work out exactly how far they still had to drive before Modesto.

"OK, looks to be… umm…" His eyes flicked back and forth from the scale to the knotted, winding roads that wove their way through the mountains. "I'd guess it's something like… If it's an inch to ten miles, then…" He whispered a few numbers under his breath as he ran a finger along the road, then he stopped, reached up and switched off the light.

"OK, maybe counting in fingers is simpler."

Cathy smirked. "Told you so. There's no point trying to work out the distance on these roads." She started to fold the map. "I used to drive this way down to Reno with my dad all the time when I was a kid, and the roads twist about so much that half the time you're headed back the way you came. The rule is you just keep going until you see a mountain you don't recognize, then you know you've missed your turnoff."

"Then I guess we'll have to play it your way," Jack reluctantly agreed. "I've never been to this corner of the state. So, you see anything you don't recognize yet?"

"Well… I mean, it's nighttime. We always drove during the day, so right now your guess is as good as mine." She looked out the windshield ahead and frowned. "Though now you mention it," she pointed out the window at the glow of lights a couple of miles down the road, "that looks like a town up ahead."

"Looks like it, yeah. Is that a problem?"

"Ummm… well, it's been a few years since I've passed this way, but I don't remember ever seeing a town this side of the lake. Hang on, let me just check the map again." She stared at it as if she were trying to read a foreign language, slowly mouthing the names of the towns along the road.

"Hold up a sec," Garside cheerfully called back from the driver's seat. "It looks like we've finally stumbled on a spot of good luck." A curve straightened in the road ahead, and playing against the trees on either side were red and blue flashing lights. "You can always rely on a policeman for decent directions."

Jack and Cathy both craned over the front seats to look out the windshield. A few hundred yards ahead they saw the cop car parked at an angle, blocking half the road, and Garside began to slow as the car flashed its headlights twice.

"I'm not sure I like the look of this," Jack muttered, watching the car with suspicion. "Are you sure we want to stop here?"

"What? Of course we want to stop!" Garside spluttered. "It's the police. Do you want me to just roar past without so much as a by your leave? This isn't Smokey and the bloody Bandit!"

"OK, Doug, settle down. I'm just saying that it's the middle of the night on an isolated mountain road, and we don't really know what's going on. Maybe we shouldn't just automatically assume the cops are still playing for our team, know what I mean?"

Garside harrumphed. "Well, I'm the person behind the wheel, and I'm stopping. If you want to let paranoia get the better of you then I suppose that's up to you, but I'm not willing to let society and common courtesy fall by the wayside, and that's that."

"OK, OK, we can stop," Jack replied. "Just… keep your foot over the gas. And maybe keep the doors locked? Just as a precaution, OK?"

After a few moments of indecision Garside reluctantly flipped the central locking, making it clear with his body language that he was only doing it to settle Jack's nerves. As he pulled up alongside the cruiser he rolled down his window and waited with the polite, innocent smile of a man who'd never met a cop in a bad mood on the graveyard shift.

"Good evening, officer," he called out, as a man climbed with what looked like great difficulty from the driver's seat. "I say, I wonder if you might be able to help us with directions. I'm afraid we seem to have gotten ourselves a little turned around."

The cop waddled slowly to the truck, his almost perfectly spherical paunch straining against the hardest working shirt buttons ever to grace a uniform. His face glowed pink from his thinning buzz cut down to the spare chins gathered above his collar, and when he finally reached the car he leaned against the door as if it was an effort to stand.

"Evening, folks," he said, slightly out of breath. He peered in through the window and noticed Cathy. "Ma'am. Hey, what's that accent? Is that some kinda British?"

Garside smiled. "Why, yes it is. Cambridgeshire, as a matter of fact. Douglas Garside, how do you do?"

A broad smile spread across the cop's face as he enthusiastically shook Garside's hand. "Boy, my wife would just eat you up. She loves that show, you know, with the fancy Brits? Downford something?"

Garside let out a dismissive snort. "Downton Abbey, I believe."

"Yeah, that's the one, Downton! Gosh, it's just her favorite show in the world. One time the TiVo forgot to record an episode, and I swear she still shoots that box the evil eye whenever she walks past. I don't mind saying, she'd just flip her lid if she met you. I don't think she's ever met a real life Brit before." He thrust his head almost entirely through the window and looked to the rear seats. "Are you folks all Brits?"

Jack leaned between the seats and held out a hand. "Sorry, no such luck. Cathy's from Oregon, and I'm from San Francisco. Jack Archer, nice to meet you."

The cop took Jack's hand, visibly disappointed. "Well, I guess Oregon's OK, but I can't say I much care for San Francisco. Too many hills for my legs. Oh, I'm Sheriff Parsons, by the way. Bill Parsons. Welcome to Plumas Creek."

"Plumas Creek?" Cathy muttered to herself from the back seat. "Can't see that on the damned map." She leaned forward, craning over the passenger seat. "Can you tell us where we are, Sheriff? We were looking for the turnoff to the 89 at Lake Almanor, but I don't know if we already passed it."

Parsons stood up, hiked his pants an inch and looked back the way they'd come. "The 89? Yeah, you passed it a good fifteen, twenty miles back. You gotta keep a look out for the sign, 'cause you won't see the lake in the dark."

"Twenty miles? Damn," Jack cursed, wishing he'd woken up sooner. If he'd been awake and looking for the turnoff they'd have been an hour further along the road by now. An hour closer to Emily.

"How about gas stations?" he asked. "We haven't seen one for a while and we're almost empty. Can we find gas on the 89?"

Parsons scratched his nose, setting his chins wobbling. "Well yeah, but…" He leaned in through the window and took a look at the gauge. "Oh boy, you're not kidding. From here it's about forty, fifty miles to the station at Greenville. You'd be cutting it real close if you try to get there on fumes. There's no need to risk it, though." He jerked a thumb behind him. "We got a Mobil right here in town. Won't be open this time of night, but there's a little motel where you can bed down until morning."

Jack scowled. "Thanks, but we're really in a hurry. My wife and daughter are waiting for me in Modesto, and we can't afford to take a break. I guess we'll have to take our chances on the 89."

"That's your call, but you won't have much luck tonight. It don't open until nine or ten in the morning, or whenever Jake Preston decides to roll out of bed. You're in the country, son. We don't exactly run on your twenty four hour city schedule." He scratched his belly and glanced at his watch. "The Mobil opens at nine, so you won't lose much time if you take a rest."

Garside turned to the back of the car. "I could do with a few hours sleep, if I'm honest. I've been on the go since this morning."

Cathy nodded. "And I wouldn't say no to pancakes for breakfast, as long as cash is still good. Sheriff, you got a diner in town?"

Parsons laughed and shook his head. "No need.

My place is right by the motel, and I'm sure Joan would be happy to cook up a royal feast for the chance to hobnob with a real Brit." He shook back his sleeve and checked his watch. "I'm headed back into town right now. You want to follow me in?"

"That sounds lovely," Garside beamed. "We'll be right behind you."

Parsons tapped the side of the car cheerfully. "Hot damn. You're gonna be a real hit at the breakfast table!" He strode back to his car with a spring in his step, and Garside turned to Jack still smiling.

"Oh, ye of little faith, Mr. Archer," he chuckled, wagging a finger. "I told you it'd all work out for the best. You just need to be a little more trusting."

Jack slumped back in his seat, watching Parsons as he climbed back into his cruiser and grabbed his radio. He spoke a few words into the handset before gunning the engine and turning the car towards town.

"Yeah," he said, feeling a shiver of apprehension. "We'll see."

CHAPTER THIRTEEN
MOMMY WON'T WAKE UP

RAMOS STARED OUT at the road ahead through bleary, red rimmed eyes, tapping out a rhythm on the steering wheel just to keep himself awake, but it wasn't working. He could feel the lead weights attached to his eyelids growing heavier with each passing minute, willing him to close his eyes and take a rest.

What he really wanted to do was crack open a window and feel the cold air on his face, but he knew it was a risk he couldn't afford to take. Without knowing which direction the high altitude winds were blowing there was no way to tell if they were still in middle of the fallout zone. Even with San

Francisco far behind them, a breath of fresh air could still be fatal.

He felt like he was barely holding on. It had been years since he'd pulled an all nighter, and even as a fresh faced, eager young doctor he'd never been any good at burning the midnight oil. He'd always been a mug of cocoa and bed by ten kind of guy, and happy with it. Now the sky was turning a lighter shade of blue to the east, and he knew that soon enough the sun would creep over the horizon and he'd have to face another grueling day. The one that was just now ending felt like it had lasted at least a week.

Karen and Emily had been sleeping fitfully for a couple of hours as Ramos wove the Prius along the half blocked highway to Sacramento. A couple of times he'd been tempted to wake them, just for the company, but he knew they were weak. If they were going to survive they needed their rest, so he settled for the unsatisfying company of the static hiss from the radio.

It seemed all the local stations were down on the FM band, even though the power was still on all the way east of Oakland. Ramos was no good with technology, but he'd stabbed randomly at the radio with his fingers until it finally began to scan through the frequencies, and so far the only thing he'd picked up was a few seconds of what sounded like a Spanish language station. A hushed, urgent voice had drifted in for a moment, but before he could make out a single word it had drifted away, replaced once more by the familiar, lonely static hiss.

He stared at the radio, willing it to produce a voice from the ether. *Any* voice, saying anything. A farmer's auction calling out beef prices. An androgynous teen singing some Godawful pop song. Hell, at this point he'd take Gilbert Gottfried and Bobcat Goldthwait screeching a duet of *Endless Love*, just so long as that damned static went away. He was sick to the back teeth of–

"*Shit!*"

His eyes returned to the road just in time to see the back of a truck looming up towards the car, and he slammed the brakes so hard it felt like his foot might punch through the floor. The Prius slowed so quickly it seemed as if the back wheels jumped from the road as the front dug in to the asphalt, and after just a few seconds the car came to an undignified stall rather than a dramatic screeching halt, just a couple of feet shy of the back of the truck and a sudden, painful death.

"Holy crap, that was close!" Ramos gasped, his knuckles white where he gripped the steering wheel.

Already he was kicking himself for his stupidity. He knew this was his fault. He was barely keeping his eyes open, barely watching the road, and it was nothing but sheer luck that he hadn't plowed into the back of the truck and killed them all. He angrily pushed open the door and climbed out of the car, amazed to see that through the panicked, squealing stop Karen and Emily hadn't even stirred from their sleep.

"Get it together, Cesar," he hissed to himself, slapping his cheeks. "There are no ambulances out here if you screw up." He leaned against the car and took a deep breath, waiting for his heart to stop racing, and it was only when he finally felt the fresh air begin to calm him down that he took a look out at the road ahead.

The truck was just the last in a long line of vehicles crowding this side of the highway, and as Ramos walked around its side he saw the extent of the blockage and cursed. There was no way through. As far as the eye could see the highway was jammed with abandoned vehicles, hundreds of them crowding all five lanes. Even the shoulder was packed. There were vehicles abandoned on the steep grass verge that looked like they'd tried to climb away from the road entirely, only to get bogged down.

This must have been the first wave of the evacuation, he realized. Back when the news first broke there must have been... *Jesus*, hundreds of thousands of people must have followed the advice to head east out of the city on the 80, all of them trying to make it to the safe zone. The road couldn't possibly handle that kind of traffic, and this had been the inevitable result. Barely fifty miles from San Francisco the artery had become completely blocked.

Ramos scanned the cars for signs of movement in the early pre-dawn light, but it only took a glance to see that there was nothing. Folks hadn't camped out in their cars, waiting for the road ahead to clear. They'd climbed out and continued on foot, and it was hardly surprising. The mushroom cloud looming over the city would have been visible even here. If there was one thing that would convince thousands of people to abandon their beloved cars and run in the other direction it was a nuclear explosion behind them.

He trudged back to the Prius in a foul mood. He'd been praying that the authorities had managed to keep the 80 clear all the way to the safe zone, wherever it was. With an open road they could have made it as far as Reno in less than four hours, but now…

Hell, he didn't even have a map. Even if he knew which way they were going it'd take the best part of a day to make it that far on the back roads. There was no telling if either of the girls could survive that long without treatment, and he knew for damned sure he couldn't keep himself awake long enough to make the distance.

With a deep sigh he slumped back into the driver's seat and pulled closed the door as quietly as he could manage, but as he started the engine he heard movement behind him.

"Doctor Ramos?" a quiet little voice asked. "Are we still on the bridge?"

Ramos twisted around in his seat and replied in a whisper. "No, honey, not any more. We're going to find medicine for you and your mommy."

Emily nodded, relieved. "Good. I didn't like it on the bridge. That man scared me."

"I know, honey, he scared me too. It's OK, though, we left him behind. It's just us now, and you're perfectly safe. How are you feeling?"

"Umm…" Emily seemed to consider the question for a moment. "A little better, I guess. My tummy doesn't hurt any more."

Ramos smiled. "Well that's great. That means you're getting better. We were a little worried about you back there."

Emily looked up at her mom, stirring a little in her sleep. "Is mommy feeling better too?"

Ramos looked at Karen, slumped forward against her seatbelt and so pale she appeared almost translucent. The only color in her face came from the inflamed pink around her nose and eyes, where her skin was so raw it looked like it had been scrubbed with wire wool. "I'm sure she's feeling better, yeah. She's just having a little nap until we get to where we're going, so let's be quiet as mice, OK? We don't want to wake her up."

Emily pursed her lips together and nodded, and with a comforting smile Ramos turned back to the wheel and began to guide the Prius back the way they'd come. He remembered passing an off ramp about a mile back along the highway, and he just prayed the roads at ground level wouldn't be as jammed up as the highway. He knew Karen wouldn't be able to walk in her condition.

By the time they reached he'd guided the car back to the off ramp the sun had begun to peek above the horizon. The Prius cast a long shadow on the empty asphalt, and in the golden dawn light Ramos felt a sudden burst of energy. He knew it was only a fleeting high, just a quick rush of optimism now that the darkness was being banished for another day, but he prayed it would be enough to keep him going until he figured out some sort of plan.

For now, though, they'd just keep driving east toward the rising sun. Sooner or later they'd reach some kind of civilization. They'd find people, doctors, medicine, equipment... they'd find *relief*, and he wouldn't have to bear the weight of caring for Karen and Emily alone. Just the thought of being able to relieve himself of the responsibility and collapse into a bed was enough to make him almost giddy.

He turned the Prius in a wide arc and powered down the off ramp, overjoyed to find that the road beyond the highway was almost completely clear. There were a few vehicles abandoned here and there, but they weren't snarled up in bumper to bumper traffic. It looked like they'd just run out of gas.

On a steel frame above the street Ramos saw signs

pointing to Dixon, Allendale and Batavia. He had no idea where any of those places were, whether they were five miles away or a hundred, small villages or large towns, but right now he didn't give a damn. They were *options*. That was all that mattered. As long as there was a clear road ahead they could drive anywhere they pleased, and he had faith that sooner or later some kind of plan would present itself.

"Ummm, Doctor Ramos?" Emily whispered, leaning between the front seats.

"Yes, honey?"

"Did you give mommy a haircut while I was sleeping?"

Ramos frowned. *What kind of a question was that?* He almost laughed as he answered. "No. Why do you ask?"

Emily held her tiny hand over the driver's armrest, and when she opened her fingers Ramos felt his heart sink.

She was holding a bundle of blonde hair in her fist. Karen's hair.

"It's OK, honey," Ramos assured her. "It's just… it's nothing, don't worry about it." Without thinking he pressed his foot a little harder on the gas.

"Mommy? Mommy, are you OK?" In the back

Ramos could hear Emily shake her mother. "Doctor Ramos, mommy won't wake up."

"It's OK, honey." Now his voice wasn't even convincing enough to fool a seven year old. "She just really needs to rest. Let her sleep."

He felt the panic constrict his throat now. His heart began to thump in his chest, and he was ashamed to realize that his first thought was entirely selfish.

If Karen dies I'll have to take care of the little girl.

He cursed himself for it, but he knew it was true. Jack was probably dead, and if Karen didn't survive he'd be stuck trying to live through a nuclear holocaust with a seven year old in tow, like an escort mission in a video game that lasts a lifetime. He just wasn't ready for that kind of responsibility. He didn't know how to keep a kid alive.

In the back seat Emily began to cry, still shaking Karen by the shoulder. "*Moommyyyy,* please wake up, I'm scared!"

Ramos ran a red light and barreled across a deserted crossroads, the weedy engine of the Prius whining in protest as he jammed the gas pedal into the floor. Now he knew where he needed to go. It was far from perfect, but he'd take any port in a storm, and right now he knew that port lay about a half mile ahead, in a sprawling mess of low flat-roofed buildings surrounded by a parking lot that looked large enough to hold every car in the state.

As he approached the lot and screeched through the entrance he saw what he was hoping to find. What he *knew* he'd find, because this lot was pretty much identical in every town across America.

In amongst the fast food joints dotted around an enormous Safeway store he saw the glowing sign he needed, and he gunned the car towards the front door.

Rite Aid Pharmacy

•▼•

CHAPTER FOURTEEN
DE NADA

THE SOUND OF footsteps and chatter on the other side of the door roused Jack reluctantly from sleep. He grunted and turned away, bending his pillow over his head to block out the noise, but against the deathly silence of the motel room it sounded like there was a carnival marching by in the street outside. A child wailing for her mother cut through his slumber like a bucket of ice water over the head, and Jack knew he wouldn't be getting any more sleep.

He peeled open one eye, and for a moment the usual bout of bleary eyed confusion hit him full in the face. He could see nothing. The room was pitch black. He had no clue where he was, but thanks to the regular blackout drinking and constant travel this had been pretty much the status quo for the last year of his life. He woke up most mornings with the same sense that wherever he was it wasn't where he was supposed to be, so often that the confusion barely worried him any more. He knew he'd just have to wait a minute for the message to get through to his brain that his body was awake.

All he remembered right now was that he was in some sort of hotel room, and even if his memory had been a *complete* blank he could have figured that out in pitch darkness. It was obvious.

All hotel rooms carried the same basic DNA. The pillow beneath his head, built more for stamina than comfort, so firm that his ear ached a little where it had been pressed against it. The smell of cheap, mildly scented laundry detergent on thin sheets still tucked tight beneath the mattress by his feet. The clean but slightly cloying aroma of a plug in air freshener, probably hidden behind the TV or in the closet, somewhere out of sight. And below it all, faint but never quite perfectly hidden, the lingering odor of the thousand people who'd used his bed before him. It was a smell no detergent could quite banish, and no air freshener could completely mask. Every hotel room had that same smell, from roadside flop houses to five star suites.

Jack pushed back the sheets and dragged himself up to the edge of the bed, and two thoughts struck him right away. First he felt a moment of disbelief when he realized that it was only yesterday he'd awoken in his hotel room in Seattle. He remembered grabbing the vodka from the mini bar. The taste of the macadamias he'd forced himself to swallow. The cold tile of the bathroom floor against his bare feet.

Has it really only been a day? It seemed like a month ago.

The second thought followed close behind, and this one was a little more pleasant.

I'm not hungover.

He thought about it for a moment, but in this half-awake fog Jack genuinely couldn't remember the last time he'd woken in a hotel room without even a hint of a headache. He couldn't remember the last time he'd woken without dragging himself to the minibar to rinse the taste of old booze from his mouth with fresh booze, but now… he didn't want to jinx it, but all he wanted right now was pancakes.

Jack scanned around the dark room, still waiting for his memory to seep back. He couldn't remember the layout of the room, and in the darkness he could only make out the dim edges of furniture. The only light he could see was the red glow cast by the digital clock on the nightstand, and he frowned as he read the time: 10:17.

AM or PM?

Now it started to come back to him, just fragments as his brain pieced together the muddled memories it managed to dredge up. He remembered rolling into town behind Parsons. He remembered the sheriff waking a maid in the motel reception. He remembered feeling so tired that he almost floated across the parking lot to his room. A couple of awkward moments as Parsons tried to politely ask without actually asking whether Jack and Cathy would be bunking together. Boomer trailing after Doug like a lovesick puppy, and Doug halfheartedly pushing her away from the door before he finally gave up and let her in. He remembered… something about his clothes? Someone tried to take them from him? He'd been so tired he barely knew what was going on.

That was… he thought about it for a moment, trying to get it straight in his head. That was just last night, right? Hell, it was just a few hours ago. *How come it's still dark?*

He pushed himself away from the bed and stumbled towards what he thought was the door, and he'd only taken a couple of steps before he began to regret it. All the little aches he'd felt yesterday seemed to have unionized while he slept. They'd ganged up into one big ache, and they were making angry demands. *Everything* hurt. He had no idea how, but even his hair seemed to sting.

"You're getting old, Jack," he told himself, limping with pain as he blindly reached out for a door handle that seemed to have shifted several feet across the wall in the night. Eventually he found it, and when he pulled open the door the blinding light was enough to send him stumbling two steps back.

"Jesus wept!" he cursed, shielding his eyes from the morning sun. He hadn't been ready for it, and it was only now the light was flooding in that he realized why the room had been so dark. There were thick blackout curtains shrouding the window. He yanked them open, forcing his eyes to acclimatize to the brightness, and as the shock began to fade he looked down and gave himself a wincing once over, painfully assessing the damage of the previous day.

It wasn't pretty. Across his chest and shoulders the

skin was grazed and bruised where the straps of the parachute had cut into him. Both elbows were crusted with dried blood, and his right thigh all the way from his waist down to the knee glowed red with road rash, probably caused when the chute had dragged him across the field. His heels were red raw where the blisters had burst from all the walking, and he had a dozen random purple and yellow bruises dotted across his body, all of them caused by God knows what. They could have come from anywhere, but all that was certain was that they all hurt like a motherf–

"Knock knock," a sing song voice called out from the door, and a figure leaned in through the gap. "Oh, sorry!" she cried, quickly pulling the door half closed when she noticed Jack. "I can come back later."

Jack looked up to find a young Hispanic maid standing just outside the room. She tried to keep her eyes politely pointed to the parking lot, but Jack could see a blush creep up to her face as he caught her sneaking a quick glance through the gap in the door. It took him a few moments to realize that he was only wearing a pair of boxer shorts.

"Oh! Sorry, don't mind me." He looked around

the room, but all he could see was his ruined suit jacket in a heap on the floor. "I don't... ummm, I don't seem to have any clothes."

"That's OK, I have them here," the maid replied, averting her gaze as she thrust a set of hangers through the gap in the door. "Mrs. Parsons washed them last night."

"Thanks, umm...?"

"Oh, Gabriela," she answered.

"Thanks, Gabriela." Jack grabbed the pants first, sliding them on before pulling the door fully open.

"Mrs. Parsons said she managed to get the worst stains out of the pants and shirt, and she asked me to give you this." She held out a green windbreaker, the chest embroidered with a Plumas County Sheriff's Department patch. "She said it used to belong to the sheriff, but he doesn't need it now that he's..." she stifled a smirk and tried not to laugh, "now that he's too big to zip it up."

Her words jogged Jack's memory. He'd been so tired when they'd arrived at the motel his brain had been pretty much completely switched off. He'd fallen into the bed fully dressed, but just as he was about to fall asleep a woman had knocked on the door and brusquely ordered him to strip. He'd been down to his underwear before it occurred to him to ask why, or who she was.

He reached out and took the jacket from Gabriela with a smile. "Thank you. And could you please pass on my thanks to Mrs. Parsons? I really appreciate this."

"You can tell her yourself," she replied.

Jack was taken aback. He didn't expect hotel maids to give him attitude.

"Ummm, OK," he said, for want of a better response.

Gabriela noticed the surprise on his face, and quickly corrected herself. "Sorry, my English. I mean she expects you for breakfast after you've showered, over at the blue house." She pointed across parking lot to a prim little wooden bungalow with a well tended yard out front. "I'd hurry if I were you. The food doesn't last long at Mrs. Parsons' table."

"That good, huh?" Jack asked as he tugged the shirt from the hanger.

"No, it's just…" the young woman hesitated for a moment, a slight grin flitting across her face, unsure whether she should speak. "The sheriff will eat everything if you don't take it first."

Jack chuckled. "Thanks for the warning. I'll be

right down. And thanks for the clothes, too."

"*De nada.*" Gabriela flashed a shy smile as she pulled the door closed behind her.

Jack tossed the shirt on the bed and moved through to the bathroom, where he found a stack of thick towels and a tray of toiletries waiting for him. The thought of missing out on the pancakes across the street weighed heavy on him, but it wasn't nearly enough to pull him away from the shower. It had been two days since he'd last washed, and since then he'd jumped out of a plane, dragged a man through a forest and push started a car on his own. The grime and sweat clinging to him felt like a second skin, and as he kicked off his pants and stepped into the warm stream he felt every muscle in his body relax.

Screw breakfast. He could stay here all–

Wait.

Something occurred to him as he squeezed out an entire miniature bottle of shower gel into his palm. The clock on the nightstand. It had read 10:17. What the hell were they still doing here? Parsons had said the Mobil station opened at nine. They should have been up and on the road more than an hour ago, but nobody had bothered to wake him?

He felt a flash of anger about the lost time, but he

couldn't muster the energy to feel genuinely mad about it as the grime sluiced away down the drain. The pain in his muscles melted away beneath the steaming hot spray, and as he rinsed the dirt from his hair he made his peace with it. There was still a long drive ahead, and an hour either way wouldn't make much of a difference. He could just make up the lost time on the road.

When he finally felt as clean as he could ever get he stepped out and quickly toweled himself off, suddenly aware of the growling of his stomach. Now the thought of pancakes pushed aside the urge to get straight back on the road, and in just a couple of minutes he found himself dressed, starving, and hurriedly walking across the parking lot. He hopped the white picket fence at the edge of the yard, and as he reached the open back door of the Parsons house he looked in to find a bizarre Norman Rockwell scene playing out in the kitchen.

•▼•

CHAPTER FIFTEEN
BROUGHAM AND GLENROSS

"JACK!"

PARSONS WIPED his hands on a napkin and lifted himself out of his seat before a heavily laden breakfast table. "How you feeling this morning? Come on, pull up a chair and dig in. Joan just fried up some more bacon."

Jack began to kick off his shoes, but Parsons beckoned him in. "Don't worry about your shoes, this ain't a museum. Homes are meant to be lived in. Come on, pull up a seat."

"Thank you," Jack replied gratefully, taking an open seat beside the sheriff, nodding a greeting to Doug as he enthusiastically devoured rashers of bacon on the other side of the table. Beneath the table Boomer picked up fallen scraps like a vacuum cleaner. "Everything looks delicious. Thank you, Mrs. Parsons. And thanks for washing my clothes. You really didn't have to do that."

The heavyset middle aged lady he vaguely remembered from the previous night gave him a warm smile as she set down another towering stack of pancakes. "Call me Joan. You're more than welcome, son, and may I say you're not looking quite so much like a zombie as you did last night. Honest to goodness, I thought you might be a ghost when you I saw you climb out of that truck."

"I guess I just needed a good night's sleep," Jack smiled, eyeing the pancakes. "And a decent breakfast."

"Well, help yourself to as much as you can eat," she said, patting him on the arm. "I don't need my Bill getting any bigger."

"It's just winter insulation, dear," Parsons interjected. "The winters get awful cold up here, Jack. You gotta pack on a few to make it through."

Joan let out the exasperated tut of a long suffering wife. "You've packed on enough insulation for the whole town to make it through winter, you big lump." Now she turned her attention to Doug, stacking bacon high on a thick slab of buttered bread. "So Douglas, you said your grandfather was a valet? That's like a special sort of butler, isn't it?"

Garside wiped his mouth daintily on his napkin and shook his head. "Oh, it's much more than a butler, my dear," he said, laying his accent on a little thicker than he had last night. "A butler merely manages a household, you see, but a valet – it's va-*let*, by the way, rather than the French pronunciation va-*lay* that you use here for people who fetch your car – a valet is a gentleman's personal gentleman. He's responsible for the well-being of his master, from taking care of his health and appearance to organizing his social engagements. He's equal parts assistant, confidante and even, on some occasions, bodyguard and friend. My grandfather, God rest him, was for many years valet to the third Lord Ponsonby of Brougham and Glenross."

"My, how fascinating!" Joan took a flustered breath and held a hand to her chest.

"Quite a dreadful man, I'm sorry to report," Doug confided in a low voice. "He was an incorrigible drunk and a philanderer, by all accounts, and unfortunately it often fell to my grandfather to…

well, let's just say he had to deal with the unintended consequences of his master's dalliances."

"You mean…?"

Doug nodded solemnly. "I'm afraid so. A child born out of wedlock could be quite the scandal in those days, and especially so given the complications of his position. The last thing a Lord would want is an illegitimate child claiming the right to a hereditary title, never mind his fortune, and I'm afraid… well, a valet will perform his duties without complaint, no matter how unsavory. Many a backstreet doctor made his fortune from the purse of Lord Ponsonby, if the rumors are to be believed."

Joan fanned herself with a hand, blushing. "Oh, I feel like I'm gossiping below stairs!"

"Then you should keep a watchful eye, my dear," Doug warned with a sly smile, narrowing his eyes and lowering his voice. "His Lordship was known to prey on the household staff when his appetite was piqued."

Jack chuckled as he poured syrup over his pancakes, and as Doug continued his story he turned to Parsons with a questioning look. "So how come we slept in so late?" he asked. "I thought we were going to head to the Mobil at nine."

Parsons took a bite out of a rasher of crispy bacon,

sprinkling fragments down the front of his shirt. "You were, yeah," he said, idly brushing the crumbs away, "I meant to wake you, but it turns out there's a town meeting up at the church at eleven. They gotta decide a few things, you know, what with the news and everything. Station's gonna be closed a little while longer, so I figured I might as well let you sleep in."

Jack nodded. "OK, that makes sense. But don't you need to be at the meeting? I'd hate to think we're keeping you from something more important."

"What, and miss breakfast?" Parsons let out a laugh. "No no, they'll fetch me if I'm needed. Don't you worry about it."

"OK…" Jack couldn't tell if he was just being polite. "But if you need to take care of anything please don't let us keep you. I'm sure we'd be just fine waiting for the station to open." He grabbed a fork and jabbed at the bacon. "Has Cathy made an appearance yet?"

Parsons shook his head, chewing silently until he finally swallowed his mouthful. "Damnedest thing," he said, picking something from his teeth with a fingernail. "Gabriela went to deliver fresh towels to her room this morning and found she wasn't there.

Said her bed hadn't even been slept in."

"*What?*" Jack couldn't believe he was only just hearing this. "You're saying she left?"

"Well, I guess so," he replied. "I can't think of a better explanation. It's not like this is a big town, so she hasn't just strolled off to the store." He narrowed his eyes. "Doug was saying you guys only met her yesterday, right? She was just along for the ride? I guess maybe she changed her mind about tagging along after all."

"But her truck is still parked outside! Why would she leave without it?"

Parsons shrugged. "Beats me. Maybe she decided to hitch a ride out with someone else. We had a fair few folks pass though town last night. Any one of them could have picked her up." He studied Jack's confused expression. "Look, I wouldn't waste too much time worrying about it. Young girls like that, they're flighty. They change their minds like we change our socks. Maybe it just occurred to her that it was a dumb idea to follow you guys down south when she could just head inland where it's safe, know what I mean?"

Jack finally nodded. "Well… yeah, I guess that would make sense. Still, I can't figure out why she'd leave her truck behind."

Parsons shrugged and took a bite from his toast. "Women," he said, spraying crumbs. "They're a different species. And maybe it wasn't her truck to begin with, you know? I'm guessing a lot of folks left car keys behind when they headed out to those safe zones." He waved his hand as if to brush the conversation aside. "So, you're a doctor, huh?"

Jack nodded, still distracted, wondering about Cathy. "Yeah. Well, I used to be. I'm not licensed any more, but…" A thought struck him. He hadn't told Parsons about his job. "How did you know I was a doctor?"

Parsons pointed to the kitchen counter. "Your ID. You left your wallet and phone in your pants when Joan took them for the laundry. I'm real sorry, but she didn't notice them until they came out the machine. Your cash is drying on the table, but I'm afraid your phone bought the farm. Still, it's not like there's any signal right now. I guess it was a useless brick anyhow."

Jack looked over to the counter with dismay. A few hundred dollars in bills were drying on a dish cloth, and his wallet and phone were sitting beside them.

He knew Parsons was right. The phone was useless

without a signal, but that wasn't the point. It was holding the last message he'd received from Karen. The thought that it had been wiped from existence in a washing machine… well, it felt as if she and Emily had just taken another step further away from him. He was heartbroken and angry, but he didn't want to lay it on Parsons.

"It's OK," he said. "I guess it was my fault for forgetting to take them out of my pocket."

Parsons nodded. "Still, I wish I'd checked before Joan threw your clothes in the machine. I'm real sorry about that."

The sheriff looked up at a knock on the back door, where a wiry man with a patchy attempt at a beard stood tapping his wristwatch. He dropped his toast to his plate and sighed. "Well, looks like they're playing my song. I'll be right with you, Ray," he called out to the newcomer, pushing back his chair and brushing an avalanche of crumbs from his shirt. "I guess I'd better head on up to the church and see what's going on. You and Doug stick around here and eat your fill. Joan'll take care of anything you need, just ask."

"Yeah, thanks," Jack replied, distractedly. "We'll be just fine."

"Then I'll catch up with you in a little while." He

turned to his wife. "Honey, you take care of these boys for me. I'll be back in an hour or so."

Joan gave him a hurried goodbye and returned to her conversation with Doug, who was spinning some unlikely yarn about a distant relative of his being thirty seventh in line for the throne. Jack returned to his breakfast as Parsons left by the back door, deep in whispered conversation with the man.

He couldn't put his finger on it, but as he poked at his cooling pancakes he suddenly felt a strange sense of unease. It was the same feeling he often had in bars in less respectable parts of town, where men passed illicit substances to each other in dark corners and women plied their trade on the street outside. It was the tense feeling of his brain whispering to him, *watch yourself,* warning him to make this his last drink.

There was something prodding at his mind, like a tongue at a loose tooth, but just as it seemed set to become clear it began to float away again, maddeningly close but just out of reach. It was... it was something about his phone. Some memory from last night, a half remembered snapshot of a moment caught by a half asleep mind.

He dropped his fork to the plate and leaned back,

his stomach full and his mind clouded by a near fatal overdose of carbs and sugar. He suddenly felt like he needed a breath of fresh air, just to clear his head.

"I'm gonna go take a walk for just a minute," he said, pushing back his chair, but it was clear that neither Joan nor Doug had heard him. She was too busy listening with rapt attention to whatever story he was weaving about centuries of bizarre, inbred English aristocracy.

Jack scooped up his phone and wallet from the counter, slipping the still damp bills into the breast pocket of his shirt to dry. The rest he tried to tuck into his jacket pocket, but then he remembered that he was wearing the sheriff's windbreaker, not his suit jacket. He ran his hands down the sides and realized there were no pockets there, so he dropped the phone and wallet in his pants pockets, stepped out onto the porch and arched his back, taking a deep breath of the cool air.

Now he looked around properly for the first time since they'd arrived. Plumas Creek looked to be a small town. Barely a village, in fact. Aside from the motel all he could see were maybe fifty or sixty small homes, neat little boxes tightly clustered in a small suburb of three or four streets. The Mobil station was visible just a few dozen yards up the road, partially hidden in the trees, and on the far side of the houses he could see the spire of a small wooden church a couple hundred yards to the south. To the north was a steep hillside covered in a thick growth of ponderosa pine trees.

Apart from that there was nothing. Plumas Creek was just a small settlement perched up in the hills, with a single road leading in and out. It was hard to tell what anyone up here might do for a living, but the motel suggested that tourism might be a part of it.

Jack made his way across the parking lot to his room, and as he stepped inside and saw his bed he was suddenly overcome with fatigue, no doubt the result of eating a stack of pancakes as big as his head. After months of surviving on the thin gruel of hotel minibars he wasn't accustomed to eating quite so well, and even though he'd only awoken an hour ago the prospect of a nap seemed inviting. He kicked off his shoes, dropped to the bed and grabbed the TV remote, flicking on the set.

There was only static and color bars on every channel. The set was an old CRT with rabbit ears sticking out the top, and Jack couldn't see anything nearby that might be a digital receiver. He squinted at the set, and he almost laughed out loud when he saw that there was a VCR player built in beneath the screen.

"What decade am I in?" he muttered to himself, flicking off the TV and tossing the remote to the bedside table.

He turned to his side, trying to find a comfortable position on the firm, spongy pillow, but however he moved it seemed that comfort was always just out of reach. It barely felt like a pillow at all, but an armrest pulled from a sofa, firm and unyielding. Eventually he gave up, pushed it aside and rested his head on a crooked arm until he felt halfway comfortable.

It was still nagging at him. Something about... *God, why can't I think straight?* Was it Cathy's disappearance that was bothering him? He thought about it for a moment, and... no, that wasn't it. It unsettled him, sure. He still couldn't figure out why on earth she'd decided to leave without saying goodbye, or taking her own truck, but when it came down to it he'd only known the girl a few hours. Hell, he didn't even know her last name. For all he knew she could have been crazy. There didn't seem much point worrying about her.

No, it was something else. Jack stared at the floorboards, trying to clear his mind to allow the thought to creep to the forefront, as elusive thoughts so often do when you just stop thinking about them for a while. He let his eyes trace the intricate, flowing patterns formed by the grain of the wood, all the way from the door to the foot of the–

That was it.

Jack sat bolt upright in the bed, a sudden chill shivering down his spine as he remembered what Parsons had said back in the kitchen.

"I'm real sorry, but she didn't notice until they came out of the machine."

When it came to his belongings Jack was a creature of habit. Functioning alcoholics usually are. They know they can't trust themselves to keep track of everything after the booze has started to seep into the blood, so they develop systems. Routines. Little habits to keep their little world ticking over, habits that became so ingrained in the mind of a drunk that they'd still follow them even if they'd forgotten their own name and couldn't walk straight anymore. Even if they suspected that the warm patch in their crotch might be the result of an accident.

Jack stared down at the floor, at the ruined suit

jacket sitting in a heap beside the bed. The right arm was torn off, and what remained was covered in so many tears and stains it was only good for dish rags, but the silk lining was still intact.

He leaned over and scooped it from the floor, shaking it out and pulling open the left lapel. There, sewn into the lining, was a discreet slanted pocket, the perfect size for his cellphone. On the other side was its twin, this one just large enough for a slim wallet with a couple of cards and a few bills.

He always kept his things in those pockets. *Always.* The habit was so ingrained he'd reach for those pockets in his sleep. His pants pockets were too shallow for his brick of a phone in any case.

He felt the hairs stand up on the back of his neck as he realized what this meant.

Someone had been in his room.

Someone had taken his wallet, and destroyed his phone. And they'd done it intentionally.

Parsons was lying to him.

•▼•

CHAPTER SIXTEEN
A SMALL MERCY

KAREN AWOKE TO yelling. Loud, furious, sharp screeching that forced her to shrink back.

"What do you mean, you won't help him?" An angry female voice rang in her ears. "You're helping *her!*"

"Ma'am, please try to understand." This was Ramos now, his voice much lower, calming and conciliatory. "I didn't say I *won't* help him. I'm saying I *can't*. I'm sorry, there's just really nothing I can do for him now."

"You mean there's nothing you can do now you've given *her* all the good medicine!" A fist slammed against a surface. "Why the hell does she get to live and my Ron dies? Who the hell gives you the right to play God?"

Karen pried open her eyes, crusted with sleep, and squinted at the bright strip lighting in the ceiling above her. She was… well, she didn't know where she was. The floor was hard and cold. The lights were blinding. Her vision was blurry. She'd swear she was imagining it, but just a few inches from her face she saw the shiny plastic faces of a dozen smiling babies staring back at her, glassy-eyed.

"Doc?" Her voice cracked, and after just one word she doubled over in a coughing fit that robbed her of breath. Her ribs stabbed at her. Each new jolt of pain brought on another another spasm, another cough, and after just a few seconds she was gripped with panic. She was suffocating.

Through tear filled eyes Karen saw Ramos appear at her side, holding a bottle of something to her lips. "You're OK, you just need some water," he said, as another cough sent the first mouthful spraying. "It'll pass, Karen, just relax. Take your time. You'll find your breath."

The second mouthful made it all the way down her throat, though the burning sensation as it went down made it feel as if she'd aspirated at least half of it into her lungs. Ramos tipped the bottle again, and finally the coughing began to subside enough to let her take a ragged breath.

"Where...?" *Where's Emily,* she wanted to ask, but her throat gave up before she could manage it. Just speaking a single word felt like her throat was full of razor blades.

"It's OK," Ramos assured her. "Everything's OK. You're both going to make it. You're safe."

Karen still couldn't see anything clearly, but behind Ramos she saw a shape approach down the... aisle? *Am I in a supermarket aisle?* It was a woman, but Karen could only tell by the sound of her voice. She was just a blurred lump through Karen's tear filled eyes.

"Well if she's gonna be OK she doesn't need all this stuff any more!" the woman yelled, her voice high pitched and frantic. "Get it out of her!" she demanded.

Ramos turned back to her, his voice climbing in volume to match hers. "You don't understand!" he insisted. "*Stop!* None of this will do him any good. I'm sorry."

The woman came closer, and Karen felt Ramos pull her towards him, shielding her from... the attack? *Is this an attack? Is she attacking me?*

"Save my Ron!"

The looming shape of the woman reached down toward her, grabbed hold of something and pulled, and a moment later Karen felt a searing pain shoot through her right arm. She tried to scream as Ramos fought the woman off, but her voice didn't come. All she could do was roll up into a ball and clutch her arm.

What's happening?

It felt like she'd been stabbed in the arm, but whatever weapon the woman had used she must have left it buried beneath the skin. The pain was still there, growing, moving as if a knife was digging around all the way down until it scraped across the bone.

Ramos jumped to his feet and tried to wrestle Karen's attacker away, but as he launched himself towards her Karen felt like she'd been stabbed again. The pain was agonizing, and this time she found her voice. Her scream was deafening. She could feel it tearing her throat to shreds, but she just couldn't hold it in.

"Please stop!" Ramos cried, pushing the woman back. "Look what you're doing to her!"

Karen pulled herself into a tighter ball, desperately trying to protect herself from whatever the woman was doing, and finally the searing agony began to subside. Her attacker dropped her arms to her sides, and as Karen blinked away the tears and her vision began to return she looked up to find the woman standing above her, her shoulders heaving in great, sorrowful sobs.

"My Ron," she wept, tears flowing down her cheeks. "Please help my *Roooooooon.*"

It was only then that Karen realized what had happened. In one hand the woman was clutching a thin rubber tube that ran to a transparent bag hung from a shelf a few feet above Karen's head. The other end of the tube, she noticed with a shiver, was attached to her arm with a length of tape, and beyond that a needle that dug beneath her skin. The woman had been tugging on it, trying to tear the needle out of her arm, and from the rivulets of blood flowing across her skin it looked like she'd almost been successful.

Ramos took the woman in his arms, comforting her as he carefully slipped the tubing from her hand and dropped it to the floor. "It's OK. Come on now, it's OK," he whispered in a soft voice. "Go be with

Ron. I'll be along in a minute. I may have something that can help him."

The woman squeezed Ramos tight, her shoulders still heaving as she tried to speak. "Thank you, doctor. Oh, God bless you. *God bless you!*"

Ramos pulled away. "It's OK. Now go on, Ron needs you by his side."

She walked away, wiping away the tears as she rounded the corner and vanished, and Ramos turned back to Karen with a sigh. "I'm sorry about that. Are you OK?"

Karen tried to sit up, supporting herself against what she could now see was a display of diapers. "I'll live," she croaked, her voice still scratchy. "Doc, where are we? Where's Emily, and who the hell was that psycho bitch?"

Ramos reached out to take her arm, gently peeling away the strip of tape and sliding the needle from beneath her skin. Already her forearm was turning an angry shade of purple where the needle had been tugged back and forth.

"In order, we're in a pharmacy, somewhere near… hell, I don't know, somewhere west of Sacramento. Emily's safe and sound. She'd taking a nap out in the car. And that woman– "

"You mean she'll live?" Karen interrupted.

Ramos smiled. "Emily? Yes, she'll be fine. Her treatment was a lot simpler than yours, in fact. Just a little topical antihistamine. Tell me, did you know that Emily suffers from allergies?"

Karen frowned, confused. "Yeah, she's allergic to… to soy, and she's had a few issues with dairy the last couple of years."

"And synthetic fabrics?"

"What? I…" Karen's mouth dropped open as it dawned on her what Ramos was saying. "Doc, are you telling me that Emily doesn't really have radiation sickness?"

He nodded, smiling broadly. "Just a common allergic reaction to the cheap ass polyester in Jared's Hawaiian shirt. It gave her a rash wherever it touched her, and I guess the vomiting was just a combination of her throat closing up and a little stress. She'll be perfectly fine."

"Oh, thank God!" Karen cried, feeling a heavy weight lift from her shoulders that had been grinding her into the ground ever since the bridge. "Thank you so much, Doc. I don't know how I can ever repay you."

Ramos pointed to the end of the aisle and lowered

his voice. "Well, you can start by cutting that poor woman a little slack. She's about to lose her husband." He tore open a pack of gauze with his teeth, spitting out the wrapper as he taped a square over the bruised puncture wound on Karen's arm. "How are you feeling? Any nausea? Headache? Confusion?"

Karen shook her head. "No, I feel fine. Better than fine, actually, apart from my arm and the fact that I don't have the slightest clue what the hell is going on."

Ramos smiled. "Good. That'll be the result of my tried and tested strategy of giving you everything I could squeeze down an IV short of the kitchen sink. You'll feel on top of the world until it all wears off."

"And then?" Karen braced herself for bad news. "What happens afterwards?"

"My best guess?" Ramos gathered up a few blister packs and rolls of bandages from the floor, stuffing them into a plastic bag. "You'll live, so long as we can get you on a course of Filgrastim."

"Filgrastim?"

"It's a granulocyte-colony stimulating factor." He noticed Karen's questioning look. "Don't worry, you don't need to know the details. Your white count is too low, and Filgrastim will stop you dying from the flu while your immune system recovers."

Karen shrugged. "You're the doc, Doc. If that's what I need, sign me up. Jab it in me, or whatever you need to do."

"They don't have it here," Ramos said, helping her to her feet. "It's usually only prescribed to chemo patients, so it's not the kind of thing your average Rite Aid keeps behind the counter."

"So we still need to go to the– "

"The safe zone, yeah. That's the only place I know we'll be able to find it."

"Then OK, no time like the present. If we have to go, let's get it over with."

"First I have to take care of a patient." He began to walk in the direction of the frantic woman, but just before he reached the end of the aisle he stopped abruptly, turned back to Karen and leaned in, speaking quietly. "Hey, ummm, try not to react when you see this guy. It's... not pretty."

Karen nodded, preparing herself for whatever awaited her around the corner, but when the man finally came into view she could barely hold back a gasp.

He was lying on the ground near the counter, his

wife sitting by his side, rocking back and forth, and when she noticed Ramos she broke into a wide, manic smile. "Are you going to help him now, doctor?"

The man's eyes were wide open, staring unblinking into the bright light above, his pupils milky. He was obviously blind, but it wasn't only the blindness that shocked Karen. From the corners of his eyes the man wept blood, and at his nose and mouth a pink froth of blood, saliva and mucus bubbled gently as he took each labored breath. Karen didn't want to look at him, but she couldn't seem to tear her eyes away. She just stared at this wreck of a human being as the woman described to Ramos what had happened to him.

"He was out in the fields," she said, as Ramos gently took the man's pulse and made a show of fussing over him. "You know, getting ready to bring in the artichokes for the season. He said he saw the flash over the city, but I guess he watched it too long because he said his eyes started to go funny when he was halfway home. All swimmy, he said. That's why he had to leave the tractor behind, you know? I found him down at the Woodrow farm just wandering around, couldn't see a damned thing. Lord knows what would have happened to him if I'd not been home."

Ramos reached deep into his plastic bag and withdrew a glass vial and a syringe, popping the foil cap with the needle. Beneath him the man moaned with pain. Ramos touched him gently on the shoulder, and then quickly turned his head to one side as his stomach convulsed and he vomited a frothy red-brown liquid.

"Do you think he'll get better, doctor?" his wife asked, using her sleeve to carefully wipe clean her husband's mouth. "It's just… well, I don't know how I'd be able to manage on my own. The farm's too big for one person, and Lord knows you can't find the help these days."

Now Karen got a good look at her she could see that the woman wasn't doing so well, either. Her eyes were sunken, and her skin was so pale it was almost translucent. After her own experience of radiation sickness it seemed that this woman had taken a larger dose.

Ramos drew a clear liquid from the vial into the syringe. He didn't seem able to look the woman in the eye, but he finally responded to her question with a non-answer.

"This will help with his pain," he said, taking the man's arm and rolling up his sleeve. He tapped the skin of his forearm until a vein appeared, and then slid the needle in. A cloud of blood swam into the clear liquid of the syringe, and Ramos prepared to squeeze the plunger.

"Wait," he said, his thumb freezing in place. "You said he drove his tractor home? From near the city?"

"Well, halfway home," the woman nodded. "Like I said, he had to stop when his eyes started to go."

"Which city are you talking about?" Ramos demanded.

The woman looked at him as if he was simple. "Sacramento, of course. The city that had a great big bomb dropped on it!"

Ramos looked up at Karen, his expression grim. "They hit Sacramento? Jesus, we were about to drive straight through there."

He returned his attention to the syringe, staring at it as if he were psyching himself up. Eventually he looked up at Karen. "Could you... could you please go to the car and get ready to leave? There are some fresh clothes waiting for you on the driver's seat. I just want to take a minute with... I'm sorry, what was your name, dear?"

"It's Marjorie," the woman replied. "Marjorie Gorman."

"I just want a moment with Marjorie." He looked back to Karen and gave her an almost imperceptible nod, then turned back to the woman. "Shall we say a prayer for Ron, Mrs. Gorman?"

Karen made her way to the door as Ramos and Marjorie bowed their heads over Ron. She had no idea why he wanted her to leave, but she didn't mind. She didn't want to spend another moment in there, staring down at the *there but for the grace of God* versions of herself. Both Marjorie and Ron were reminders of the hell she'd narrowly escaped, and just how close she'd come to death.

Karen knew that with just a little more exposure to the fallout she too would have been lying on the floor bleeding from her eyes. Right now she could be laying there in agony, praying for the end, and as she reached the Prius and saw Emily curled up on the back seat she felt an almost overwhelming rush of gratitude that she was still on her feet and breathing.

It all hit her at once, the thought that she'd come so close not only to dying, but to losing her daughter. Escaping the city had been a million to one shot. They could have died a half dozen times along the way, and each time the difference between life and death had been nothing but the toss of a coin. The fact that they were both still alive was nothing short of a miracle.

Five minutes passed before Ramos emerged from the pharmacy to find Karen in the back seat, clutching hold of Emily as tight as she dared. It was only when Karen saw the drawn expression on his face that she set her sleeping daughter back down on the seat and climbed out of the car.

"You OK, Doc?" she asked.

Ramos walked around to the passenger side of the car, slumped into the seat and closed his eyes. His fists were clenched in his lap.

"Doc, what's up?" Karen pressed.

Ramos didn't open his eyes. He simply shook his head and muttered, "Could you drive, please?"

Karen climbed into the driver's seat, taking Ramos by the shoulder as she sat. "What happened in there, Doc? What's wrong?"

Now he finally looked at her, his eyes swimming with tears, but still he didn't speak.

"Doc? You're really worrying me now. What did you do?"

Once again he shook his head and took a deep,

shuddering breath. "Nine thousand milligrams of Secobarbital," he said. "That's the lethal dose. That's enough so he'd drift away in a few minutes. No more pain. He'd just… fall asleep."

"Doc… Please, tell me you didn't."

Ramos reached out for the window controls, rolling his down a few inches, and with a sigh he unclenched his fist. In his hand was the syringe, but the plunger was still drawn back. Clear liquid and a cloud of blood filled the reservoir. He reached up and dropped it out the window, then wiped a tear from his cheek and closed his eyes once again.

"I couldn't bring myself to press it down," he said, shaking his head. "Please just drive."

•▼•

CHAPTER SEVENTEEN
FIGHT OR FLIGHT

JACK STEPPED OUT from his room and onto the wooden porch that separated the building from the parking lot, and for a moment he just stood there, carefully taking in his surroundings as if for the first time.

Cathy's truck was still there, the only vehicle in the lot, just where Garside had clumsily parked it the night before, and on the far side of the lot was the little blue Parsons house. It had looked so inviting just a half hour ago, but now... now there was something ever so slightly off about the place. About the whole town. There was a chill Jack hadn't noticed before, but it wasn't in the air. It was something else that made the hairs on the back of his neck stand on end.

He jumped at a sudden sound to his right, a rhythmic squeaking coming from somewhere out of sight, and before he could catch himself he found his fists clenching of their own accord. He shifted his stance, preparing himself to either fight or run. His heart fluttered in his chest, and it wasn't until the maid's cleaning cart came wheeling around the corner that he realized his fingernails were digging into his palms.

Jack forced himself to relax. He took a deep breath and shook out his hands as Gabriela gave him a cheerful wave, and he managed to offer a smile in return.

"Hola," she called out. "You had a good breakfast?"

Jack nodded, taking a few steps in her direction as casually as he could manage. "Yeah, thank you, it was delicious. Just, ummm, grabbing a little fresh air now. Gotta help the old digestion. I see you're… ummm… I see you're cleaning the rooms. That's great." He cringed at the painfully stilted small talk, but it was all he could manage with his mind racing a mile a minute.

"Yes," she replied, a look of mild concern flitting across her face. "Is everything OK with your room? I can clean it now if you want."

"No, no, everything's fine," he assured her, realizing she must have thought he was criticizing her work.

Gabriela gave him an awkward smile as she reached across her cart and lifted a bunch of keys dangling from a hook on the corner. "Are you sure? I really don't mind if you need anything." She unlocked the door in front of her, the room next to Cathy's, and hung the keys back on their hook.

"No, seriously, I'm fine." Jack sidled towards her as casually as he could manage, quickly scanning the cart. "It's just... I need..."

As he reached out to the cart and grabbed a roll of toilet paper he realized that his dream of becoming James Bond was never going to come true. "Sorry, I finished the roll in my room. Thank you."

Gabriela smiled politely. "*De nada.*" The look of concern flashed across her face again, but this time it was the concern someone might feel on realizing that a guy had used an entire roll of toilet paper in just a few hours. "You can take more if you're having... a problem," she said, holding out another roll. "We have plenty."

"Thank you, I'm fine," Jack replied, awkwardly throwing her a salute with the roll in his hand. His Bond dream was quickly vanishing over the horizon. "I'll just take... this and head back to my room. Thanks for your help."

Gabriela's smile had turned almost to pity now, and she hurriedly grabbed a mop and bucket and vanished into the room to escape the awkward conversation.

"Smooth, Jack," he whispered to himself, grabbing the keys from the hook. He could feel his cheeks glowing pink with embarrassment, but there was no time to worry about that now. He rushed back to Cathy's door, flipping through the bunch until he found the right key, and then he walked on tiptoes back to the cart to replace them at the corner. Through a gap in the curtain he could see Gabriela carry the mop into the bathroom. She hadn't seen him.

He returned to Cathy's door, quickly scanned around the parking lot to make sure that nobody was watching and then slipped inside, closing the door quietly behind him.

As the door closed the room was plunged into

almost complete darkness. Jack didn't dare open the blackout curtains just in case someone happened to look through the window, so he decided to make do with what little daylight crept through from the open bathroom door at the back of the room. It wasn't much, but it was just enough to avoid tripping over the furniture.

Parsons had been right. Unless Gabriela had already made up the room sometime this morning Cathy's bed hadn't been slept in. The corners of the sheets were still tucked beneath the mattress, but they were rumpled a little where, Jack guessed, she'd sat on the bed when she arrived.

He looked around at the rest of the room, but in the gloomy darkness nothing seemed out of place. Cathy hadn't brought any luggage with her, so it's not as if he expected to find clothing strewn from an open suitcase, but he expected at least *some* evidence that she'd been here. A small part of him had half expected to find signs of a struggle, broken furniture and shattered mirrors. Maybe a telltale splash of blood on the bedsheets, but not this perfectly ordinary, slightly shabby motel room.

Am I overreacting?

Hell, maybe he *had* put his phone and wallet in

his pants pocket. He'd been exhausted when they arrived at the motel. Maybe it had just slipped his mind. And maybe Cathy *had* just decided to leave without saying goodbye. Maybe she'd decided that driving to Southern California with two strangers in the aftermath of a nuclear attack hadn't been the best idea she'd ever had. God knows she'd be right about that.

And what was the alternative? That the friendly local sheriff and his wife were really hardened criminals, intent on… what, exactly? What could they possibly want with him that would lead them to rifle through his things and intentionally destroy his phone?

Jack sat on the edge of the bed, suddenly realizing what a monumental fool he'd been. He was on edge. He was under more stress than he'd felt since the day Robbie had died, and he'd let it get to him. He'd taken a couple of perfectly innocent events and then joined the dots to create some illusory threat in his tired, addled mind, and now he was suspicious of a couple of nice, friendly people who'd done nothing but give him directions and feed him a delicious breakfast.

He just needed a little more sleep, he told himself.

Another hour or two of rest on a soft, comfortable bed then he and Garside would be back on the road, fresh air blowing through the windows and a clear road ahead. He'd be fine so long as he didn't let his imagination get the better of him. There were enough real threats out there without creating more out of thin air.

He pushed himself up from the bed, suddenly realizing he'd have a hell of a time explaining to Gabriela what he was doing in the wrong room without a key. He just hoped she wasn't out on the deck when he left. If he could just make it back to his room without her seeing him he could put all of this behind him and get on with the–

His foot caught on something as he walked towards the door, something small that skated across the floorboards until it hit the wall beneath the window. Jack dropped to his knees, determined to leave the room undisturbed, and he felt blindly across the floor until his fingers closed over an object that felt like it didn't belong.

He picked it up and lifted it into the dim light, and as he realized what it was all of his doubts came flooding back. For a long moment he stared at it, trying to process just what it meant, but his mind wouldn't cooperate. There were just too many thoughts rushing through it to make any sense from the noise.

The cacophony in his head was so loud that he almost didn't notice the real noise, just outside the door, but finally it broke through the racket.

It was the squeaking of Gabriela's cart, just outside Cathy's door.

He panicked. The room only had one door, and it was blocked. He fell back to his knees and scurried towards the bed, hoping he might be able to hide under there, but even in the darkness he could tell there wasn't enough room. The base of the bed sat low above the floor, maybe eight inches high. There was no way he could fit.

He scanned around in the dim light, desperate for options, but the sparsely furnished room offered no obvious hiding places. There wasn't even a real closet he could hide in, just a clothes rack bolted to the wall.

He could hear Gabriela now, quietly singing to herself in Spanish just outside the door, and he knew at any moment he'd hear the sound of the key in the lock. What could he do? Just bolt past her as she opened the door? Pretend he thought this was his room? Try to think up some reason he might be in here alone?

That might work, he realized, if she didn't know Cathy had already left. If she didn't know the door had been locked. There would be at least enough doubt that she wouldn't immediately scream bloody murder. He and Cathy had arrived together, after all. Why *shouldn't* he be in her room? For all Gabriela knew they could be a couple.

A chilling thought hit him.

What if Gabriela was in on whatever was going on? What would she do when she realized Jack knew that something was wrong?

No, he couldn't let her see him. She couldn't know what he'd found on the floor of the room. If he was going to buy himself the time to figure out what the hell was happening he had to get out of there, and quickly.

He fumbled through the darkness towards the second hand daylight of the bathroom. There was a window there, he knew, leading out onto the back of the building, and if it was anything like the one in his room it was just about large enough to climb through.

Jack reached the bathroom door as he heard the

metallic jangle of keys. He slipped inside and carefully closed the door behind him as he heard a key slip into the lock, and he climbed up onto the toilet as the front door swung open.

The window was already wide open, and it was just large enough to allow him to squeeze through and drop down to the narrow alleyway running behind the rooms. He lowered himself down slowly, trying to stay silent, and he winced at the sound of gravel crunching beneath his feet, but he couldn't afford to walk on tiptoes now.

He ran. He ran as fast as he could until he reached the corner of the building, and then he stopped with his back pressed against the wall as soon as he was out of sight, his heart thumping in his chest and his head swimming, staring down bewildered at the object in his hands.

He could buy that Cathy might have decided she didn't want to travel with them.

He could accept that she might have decided to leave without saying goodbye.

He could even bring himself to believe that she'd decided to leave her truck behind for them, and hitch a ride with someone else.

He could believe all of that, if he had to, but there

was one thing he couldn't believe. No matter how he turned it over in his head it still didn't make any sense.

Why would she leave without her gun?

CHAPTER EIGHTEEN
FIGURE IT OUT, JACKASS

THE NIGHT HAD been cold, and it felt like it had lasted a lifetime.

Cathy sat huddled among the ponderosa pines in the forest overlooking the town, just a hundred yards or so from the foot of the hill where the motel grounds began. Despite the warm morning sun she was still shivering in her light jacket, partly from the bone deep cold of the night that still clung to her, and partly from sheer exhaustion.

She'd been watching the motel from the cover of the forest since the early hours. She'd watched the cop, Parsons, lug his fat ass in and out a few times since before dawn, vanishing off towards the church in the distance before returning a half hour later.

She'd even watched Parsons send out what looked like a search party, and she could only guess they were looking for her. Fortunately he'd only managed to muster a few men at such an early hour, and in the cold, dark night their hearts hadn't seemed to be in the hunt. Once they'd swept the motel grounds, checked the street and ventured a few steps into the forest they'd quickly thrown up their hands and wandered off in the direction of the houses to the south, in search of a warm bed.

That had been around five hours ago, and since then Cathy had barely moved a muscle from her hiding place in the trees. She knew she was concealed well enough among the ponderosas – they'd made a perfect hiding spot in the darkness – but now that the sun was high in the sky she knew that an eagle-eyed observer might spot her through the fronds if she tried to make a move. She didn't even dare light up a cigarette for fear that the smell might drift down to the parking lot and give away her location.

Hell, it had been a cigarette that got her into this mess in the first place.

She stared down at the truck parked in front of her room, sorely tempted to make a dash for it, but she knew it would be a bad idea. Even if she could reach the truck without being seen it was almost certain that it wouldn't move an inch. Parsons had been screwing with it in the night, and while she wasn't sure what he'd done she was pretty damned certain he hadn't given it a tune up. And even if he *hadn't* disabled the truck she knew it was almost out of gas. She wouldn't make it more than a few miles out of town before she ground to a halt, and then Parsons or one of his goons would have no problem picking her up.

She'd almost run when she saw Doug wander out of his room about an hour after dawn. He'd sauntered across the parking lot without a care in the world, Boomer happily trailing along behind him, and then an hour or so later Jack followed, still tugging on his shirt, hurrying across to the blue house on the other side of the parking lot.

That's when she'd figured it out. *They still didn't know anything was wrong.*

The realization had hit her like a half brick to the face. For hours she'd waited, shivering, for the guys to wake up and figure out what was happening. She'd expected them to cotton on quickly when they discovered she wasn't in her room. She'd assumed they'd find her truck, the keys still hanging from the ignition, and then find her room empty. Surely then it would be obvious that something bad was going down.

But no. From Cathy's vantage point in the forest she could see straight through the kitchen window of the blue house, and even though they were tiny at this distance she was sure she could make out Doug and Jack enjoying breakfast with the sheriff and his wife, as if nothing was wrong.

How the hell had Parsons explained her absence? Had Doug and Jack not heard the ruckus in the night? Had they not heard the people coming and going at all hours?

God, they must be dumb.

A little while after Jack entered the blue house Cathy watched as Parsons left with another man, one of the guys from the pre-dawn search party. They climbed back into the sheriff's cruiser and drove once again in the direction of the church.

That's when she thought about heading down there. As far as she could tell there was only the sheriff's wife still in the house with Jack and Doug, and she couldn't imagine a chubby housewife in an apron would put up much of a fight. They could tie her up if they had to, then figure out what Parsons had done to the truck, then get the hell out of Dodge before anyone knew what was going on.

And then Cathy had noticed the maid. She had no idea what part she played in all of this, if any, but she seemed to be the only member of staff working at the motel today. Surely she must be in the loop. She'd been there last night as they checked in, and she'd probably been there when Parsons sent his boys searching for Cathy.

She was almost certainly in on it, and unfortunately she looked a little more feisty than the sheriff's wife. Cathy hadn't so much as thrown a punch in ten years, and she didn't want to go toe to toe with a woman who might know how to handle herself. It was just too risky.

So now she sat, her jacket wrapped tight around her as the confusing drama unfolded on the streets below, like watching a foreign movie without subtitles. In the distance she could see people moving on foot towards the church. And now here came Jack, once again crossing the parking lot back to his room.

"Figure it out, jackass," she whispered. "These people aren't your friends."

She'd almost given up hope. She knew Jack was

walking into a trap but he couldn't seem to see it, and if he didn't work it out soon she'd have to… *what? Go down there and kick some ass?* Hell, she didn't even have her gun. She'd dropped it by the bed when she'd reached her room, and she was in such a hurry to escape she hadn't even remembered the single most valuable thing she owned when she'd run.

"Stupid," she whispered to herself. "What were you thinking, Cathy?"

A movement down below drew her eye back to the parking lot. It was Jack again, emerging from his room and looking… different, somehow. On edge. He almost jumped out of his skin as the maid emerged from her little supply closet and turned around the corner.

She watched with growing interest as Jack… flirted with the maid? That couldn't be right. From up here he seemed to be sending all the usual flirtatious signals, but she figured she must be getting the wrong end of the stick as he started waving toilet paper around like an idiot.

But then…

"Yes!" She punched the air when she saw him lift the set of keys from the maid's cart, and her excitement only grew as he ran to her room and

slipped inside. "Not so dumb after all, Jack. Good boy, you're figuring it out."

Cathy watched the motel like a hawk, counting the seconds since Jack entered her room, and her heart skipped a beat when she saw the maid reappear from the room next door much sooner than she'd expected, dropping her mop and bucket back into the cart. "You've only been cleaning a couple minutes, woman," she hissed. "It's no wonder this place looks like a crap hole."

She pushed herself off the ground and started running between the trees as the maid pushed her cart towards Cathy's room. She had no idea what she was planning to do, but if the maid was part of this she couldn't let her discover Jack. She'd have to… well, if it came to it she'd have to do whatever was necessary to keep her quiet. If that meant knocking the bitch out with a mop handle then she could make her peace with it.

Cathy ran down the hill as fast as she could, almost skating along the loose dirt and slippery layer of fallen pine needles, but even as she sprinted out of control down the slope it was becoming clear she wouldn't make it in time. She was still more than fifty yards away when the maid found the right key and slipped it in the door, frowning as she realized it was already unlocked.

Cathy opened her mouth to let out a yell. She had no better ideas. If she could just distract the maid long enough for Jack to slip out the door she might be able to–

Wait.

Just as she reached the foot of the hill Cathy saw movement in the narrow alley at the back of the building. She stopped in her tracks, still hidden among the last of the trees as she saw Jack tumble awkwardly out the bathroom window and start to run towards her, slipping across the loose gravel. He rounded the corner at the very moment the maid poked her head through the window. A fraction of a second sooner and she'd have seen him bolt around the corner, but instead she just stared out at the empty alleyway, confused, and then ducked her head back inside and closed the bathroom window.

Jack was breathing hard, obviously scared, pressed up against the wall as if he was trying to blend in with the brickwork.

And in his hand he was holding Cathy's gun.

She waved frantically to grab his attention, biting her lip to keep herself from yelling out to him, and when he finally noticed her hiding behind the treeline he froze for a moment, mouth agape, before his body finally took over from his confused brain and sent his feet running in her direction. He bolted into the forest, following Cathy as she began to climb once more to her secret spot in the pines.

"*Wait!*" he hissed, panting, a dozen steps behind her. "Stop, damn it! What the hell's going on?"

Cathy didn't have the breath to answer. She pushed on another hundred yards up the hill before she finally stopped climbing, safely hidden among the ponderosas, and she collapsed to the ground and sucked in air while Jack caught up with her. He fell down at her side in the leaf litter, still clutching the gun in his fist.

"Will you please tell me what's happening?" he gasped. "Why did you run? What do they want with you?"

Cathy shook her head, still fighting for air. She felt dizzy. Pinpricks of color exploded in her eyes as her heart raced.

"They don't want anything with me," she finally managed. "It's not *me* they want."

"Then what the hell's going on? Why are we running?"

She looked down to the motel where the maid was emerging from Cathy's room. She tossed her mop to the ground, reached into her cart and pulled out a two way radio, hissing a few words into the set as her eyes darted across the parking lot.

"Jack," she said, staring at the maid with a mixture of hatred and fear, "don't you get it?"

"Get what? I have no idea what you're talking about!"

Cathy nodded towards the house, where the sheriff's wife emerged from the kitchen and waved over to the maid. Mrs. Parsons stepped away from the door as Gabriela arrived, ensuring she was out of Doug's earshot before they started whispering back and forth. The maid jabbed a finger towards Cathy's door.

"They want *you*, Jack. They're not going to let you leave."

•▼•

CHAPTER NINETEEN
TIP YOUR DRIVER

FOR TWO HOURS Karen drove slowly north, avoiding the highway and sticking to the cracked and potholed county routes that ran arrow straight between endless acres of patchwork farmland. The road seemed to stretch out forever ahead of the car, broken only by the occasional deserted village or isolated suburb, and as Karen stared out at the road ahead she was left with nothing to occupy her but her thoughts.

The rumble of the road had quickly lulled Emily back into a deep slumber. She lay curled up on the rear seat, her knees tucked against her belly, warm and cozy in a set of pajamas Ramos had found for her at the pharmacy. Every so often she muttered in her sleep, unconsciously scratching at the ointment-slathered pink rash at her neck, but she didn't appear to be in any discomfort.

Ramos, on the other hand, looked about as uncomfortable as it was possible to be, staring blankly out the window without really seeing anything that passed by. He'd barely spoken a word since Karen had pulled out of the Rite Aid parking lot, and after a few attempts to get him to talk about what had happened Karen had stopped trying. He clearly wasn't interested in a heart to heart.

If she was honest with herself Karen had to admit that she was happy with his silence. She couldn't imagine what the Doc was going through, and even if he'd been willing to talk she wouldn't have the first clue what to say. The last thing she wanted to do was have an honest discussion about whether it would have been right to inject a dying man with enough sedative to kill him. That… well, that just didn't sit well with her.

She'd always made it a firm rule to steer well clear of the big, knotty ethical debates of the day. When she picked up the newspaper she skipped the op-eds and jumped straight to the lifestyle section where she knew she wouldn't have to deal with anything that would give her a throbbing headache, and when her friends tried to drag her into a fight over whatever was blowing up on social media she was always the first to look for the nearest exit.

It wasn't that she didn't care. Far from it. It was just that she already had more than enough on her plate without worrying about questions with no clear right and wrong answers. She was a single mother trying to hold down a full time job in a city that kept getting more and more expensive by the year, and she knew it was a waste of time to try to set the world to rights. She'd happily leave that job to politicians, activists, idealistic college students and others who didn't have to get up in two hours to do a load of laundry and pack a lunch before eight hours at the office.

Mercy killing, though?

She just didn't know how to feel about what Ramos had almost done. She'd read her Bible from cover to cover, and she'd listened to people make good points on both sides of the argument, but still she'd never been able to decide if it really was a mercy, or just a killing.

All she knew was that she was thankful it hadn't

been her holding the syringe, asked to make that impossible choice. She'd seen the man. She didn't need a medical degree to know that the rest of his short life would be filled with nothing but agony. She just didn't know if she'd be able to find the strength to push that plunger, knowing that his blood would be on her hands.

Karen played out the same arguments over and over in her head as she drove, going back and forth without ever coming close to an answer that satisfied her. As she struggled over the question she barely paid any attention to the flat, featureless landscape ahead, which made it all the more surprising when Ramos, without any warning at all, finally broke his two hour silence with a question.

"What's a city bus doing all the way out here in the sticks?"

Karen snapped out of her reverie, just as surprised to hear Ramos speak at all as she was at what he'd said. "Sorry, what was that?" she asked, certain she'd misheard him.

"That bus we just passed," he replied, pointing a thumb at the road behind them. "You didn't see the people waving us down?"

Karen slowed the Prius and twisted in her seat to

look out the back window, half expecting to see nothing but empty road back there, but sure enough Ramos was right. About a hundred yards behind them, here on a single lane country road running from nowhere to nowhere at least a hundred miles from the city, a San Francisco city bus sat by the side of the road. Standing beside it a couple of figures jumped up and down, waving frantically in their direction.

"Huh. Well there's something you don't see every day. What do you think we should do?" Karen asked. She prayed he'd tell her to drive on, but she didn't want to be the first to say it.

"I don't know. Looks like they could be in trouble." Ramos scratched his stubble, squinting back at the bus, deep in thought. "I think…" He fell silent for a moment, as if there was some internal struggle going on. "I think we need to go back and help. Scratch that. I think *I* need us to go back and help." He gave Karen a weak smile. "I could use the karma, know what I'm saying?"

"OK, Doc," Karen nodded, reluctantly steering the car onto the dusty verge to make a U-turn. She could see the pain in Ramos' eyes, and she knew he wouldn't be able to shake off the guilt of leaving that man to a painful death until he'd done an honest, simple, unambiguous good deed.

Saving a bunch of folks stranded at the side of the road? Well, it didn't get much simpler than that.

Karen slowed as she pulled the Prius alongside the bus, ready to step on the gas if she saw any signs of danger, but as far as she could tell there was nothing to suggest they were driving into an ambush. A few passengers sat hiding from the sun in the shade of the bus, weakly cheering as she pulled to a stop beside them. She rolled down her window and peered up at the sign on the side of the bus.

"The 28 to Nineteenth Avenue?" she called out with a smile. "Someone should tell the driver he's strayed a little off his route. You guys having trouble?"

A slim, attractive black woman of around forty stepped down from the bus, her short hair flecked with the same shade of gray as her Muni bus driver's uniform.

"Wait, you're telling me this isn't Golden Gate Heights? Damn it, I'm gonna get my pay docked again." She broke into a grin. "Thank you so much for stopping. We've been stuck out here for about three hours now, and everyone else just shot straight by."

"Happy to help," Karen replied, reaching out to shake the driver's hand. "I'm Karen, and this is Emily asleep in the back."

The woman took a look through the window and smiled. "Aww, ain't she a cutie?"

"And this," Karen said, "is Doctor Ramos."

Ramos leaned over Karen to make himself visible. "Nice to meet you. Now what's the... Valerie?"

The driver ducked down to look through the window, and her smile spread even wider. "Hey, Cesar!" She slapped her thighs and let out a raucous laugh. "Of all the gin joints in all the world."

"You two know each other?" Karen asked as Ramos hopped out of the Prius.

"Damn right we know each other," Valerie beamed. "Cesar rode my bus every Tuesday and Friday like clockwork for the last five years." It was too quick to be certain, but Karen would have sworn she gave him a sly wink. "Baked me cookies last Christmas, too."

Ramos began to blush as Karen stared at him with surprise. "Well, you gotta tip your bus driver at Christmas. How else do you get the good seats?" He hurried around the car and gave Valerie a hug, smiling for the first time in hours. "How you doing, Val? What do you need?" As he pulled away from the hug Karen noticed he kept hold of her hands.

"Oh, we're OK," Valerie replied, "but I think all this sun is aging me." She tilted back her head and showed him her neck. "What do you think, Cesar? Am I getting wrinkles?"

Karen climbed out of the car and lifted Emily from the back seat as Ramos grinned at Valerie. "I swear you get younger every time I see you."

"Oh, you old tease," she laughed, slapping him playfully on the shoulder. "You always tell the best lies."

Karen gave a polite cough. "Nuclear attack, you guys," she reminded them. "Maybe we can save the… whatever this is until later? Why don't you tell us how we can help?"

Ramos quickly let go of Valerie's hand, and they both suddenly looked like a couple of school kids being lectured by their teacher.

"Sorry, you're right," Valerie said, pulling away. "We just need a jump start to get us going again. The alternator's been on its last legs for a couple of weeks now. In the city we've been switching out fresh batteries until we could schedule some time for this one to go to the shop, but when they announced the evacuation I just didn't think about it. Didn't remember the batteries were draining down until we stopped for a pee break and I couldn't get her started again."

"Will a jump start be enough?" Ramos asked. "If your alternator's busted, won't the battery just drain again in a few minutes?"

"I hope not," Valerie replied. "It's a bit of a long shot, but if you can give us enough of a jolt to get the big diesel started we might be OK. Once it's going it doesn't need power to keep it running. This isn't like a regular car. I can switch off everything electrical once we're moving. God willing she should last as far as Truckee."

"Truckee?" Karen asked.

"Yeah, Truckee." Valerie looked at her as if she'd just dropped in from the moon. "The new safe zone? What, you guys didn't get the memo? They moved it out from Auburn about an hour after Sacramento got hit."

"Val," Ramos interjected, "we didn't even know it was supposed to be in Auburn. Hell, I don't even know where Auburn *is*. We haven't seen the news since... what, yesterday afternoon? Last time we saw a TV was about an hour before the bomb dropped on San Francisco."

"Oh, man, seriously? You guys are like… I don't know, like you're still on the first season of Breaking Bad while we're all watching Better Call Saul." She saw Karen shake her head, confused. "I mean you're way behind the rest of us. Doesn't your radio work?"

Ramos shook his head. "No. I mean it works, but it just picks up static on the FM band. I couldn't get any active stations."

"Jesus, so you really don't know what's been going on? Thank God I have the CB." She pointed to the cab of the bus. "I can tune in to all sorts of channels with that big ass antenna. We even picked up a couple of military frequencies last night, but they've mostly gone dark now."

"Can you tell us what's going on?" Karen asked. "We're flying blind here."

"I sure can," Valerie replied, heading towards the back of the bus, "but let's save story time until we've got this thing rolling again. Cesar, can you give me a hand?" She looked over at Karen, still carrying her sleeping daughter in her arms, and turned to one of the passengers hiding in the shade of the bus. "And you," she said, pointing to a young man, "can you pull the car around to the back? I need it up as close as you can get it. My jump leads are only about six feet long."

The young man nodded and climbed to his feet. "Keys are in the ignition?" he asked, turning to Karen.

"Yes. Thank you." Karen shifted Emily to her other shoulder and followed Valerie to the back of the bus. "Hey, where are the rest of your passengers? You didn't only evacuate with three people, right?"

Valerie shook her head as she hefted the engine cover up onto its stands. "Oh Lord, no. I had a few dozen in the back when we left the city, but most of them didn't want to chug along at jogging pace while everyone else was breaking the speed limit. I handed a few of them off when we passed an army checkpoint out near Vallejo. Those guys had some seats left in their big troop transport things. Everyone else got out in Vacaville when we stopped for water."

She smiled at the memory as she wiped the grease from the battery terminals with her sleeve. "It was nice, you know? You kind of expect people to be every man for himself when something like this happens, but folks were lining up to help. We just stopped for a minute to grab some water and about a half dozen pickups pulled up to offer space in the back. Felt like we were all in it together, know what I mean?"

She wiped her oily hands on her shirt and let out a bitter laugh. "It's changed now, of course. It's not even been a day and people are already turning mean. You know we had five cars go by in the last few hours? Five, and not a single one of them even tapped the brakes." She shook her head sadly. "Oh well, at least you guys stopped. Cesar, can you help me pull down these leads?"

Ramos reached up above the open engine bay where Valerie directed him, pulling out a long set of thickly insulated cables.

"OK, you can bring the car around now," Valerie called out. She waited a few seconds, and then called out again. "Chop chop, it's hot out here."

Karen felt her heart sink as she heard the crunch of tires on gravel.

"No," she muttered, jogging awkwardly around the back of the bus, bouncing Emily in her arms. "No, no, no, no!" She cleared the bus just in time to see wheels spinning in the dust at the side of the road. "*No!*" she cried, watching the Prius turn back onto the road. It fishtailed for a moment, the tires searching for grip on the asphalt, and then the engine kicked in as the car began to pick up speed.

"What's happening?" Valerie demanded, concern in her voice.

"They're leaving!" Karen could barely bring herself to believe what she was seeing. *"They're leaving us behind!"*

•▼•

CHAPTER TWENTY
SURVIVAL OF THE FITTEST

JACK PANTED WITH exertion, trailing a dozen steps behind Cathy as she scrambled further up the steep hillside. A thick mulch of fallen pine needles made it tough to take a step forward without his slick-soled Oxfords sending him two slides back, but Cathy had insisted.

She refused to speak until they'd climbed far enough from the parking lot that she was sure nobody down below could hear them, so Jack reluctantly climbed, and it was only when he'd dragged himself another hundred yards uphill of the little blue Parsons' house that Cathy finally fell to her knees in the shadow of a ponderosa, pulling a pack of

Camels from her jacket pocket as if they were precious treasure. Jack suspected this was the real reason she'd wanted to climb higher, but he didn't bother to press the point.

"So," he gasped, falling gratefully to the ground beside her. "Are you gonna tell me what the hell's going on, or do I have to guess?"

"Hang on, Jack." Cathy leaned into the flame from her lighter, struggling to catch the tip of the cigarette with her trembling hands. "I didn't get a comfortable bed and a nice cooked breakfast like you did," she said, finally meeting the flame. "Gimme a second to get myself together."

Jack sighed with frustration as Cathy took a deep pull on the cigarette, exhaling a cloud of smoke along with hours of pent up stress, and while she burned down half of it with a few furious draws he turned his attention back to the motel far below.

It was hard to tell from up here, but it looked like Gabriela was poking around his room. Mrs. Parsons stood in the yard of the blue house, chewing nervously on her nails as she watched the maid unlock the door and vanish inside, and when Gabriela re-emerged and shrugged her shoulders Mrs. Parsons grabbed her radio and spoke a few words. It looked like they'd figured out he wasn't there any more.

Cathy coughed. "God, I needed that. I've been dreaming about a cigarette for about six hours now. I don't suppose you have anything to drink, right?"

"Sorry, I forgot to raid the mini bar," Jack growled impatiently. "Now what did you mean when you said they're not gonna let me leave?"

"I mean exactly that, Jack." Cathy wrapped her jacket tightly around herself, shivering despite the warm sun. "They're planning to keep you here. I was down there," she said, pointing to the parking lot. "Last night. After you guys went to bed I realized I'd left my smokes in the truck, so I went out to find them. That's when I saw the… y'know, that fat woman. The sheriff's wife. The maid let her into your room."

"Yeah," Jack nodded. "She came in to take my clothes for the laundry. I remember that."

Cathy shook her head. "No, not then. That was just after we checked in. I'm talking about later, maybe a couple hours after we arrived. You were out like a light. I could hear you talking in your sleep all the way from the truck."

"You mean Mrs. Parsons went into my room while

I was sleeping?"

"Did I stutter? *Yes,* while you were sleeping. I heard her say something to the maid about forgetting your jacket when she took the rest of your clothes."

"But she didn't wash my jacket. It's still on the floor in my room, torn to shreds."

"Yeah, I know. Will you just shut up and listen? I was watching her from the truck. When she picked up the jacket she rifled through your pockets. I figured she'd drop your things on the nightstand, but when she came out of your room a minute later she was still holding your wallet and your phone. I thought she was robbing you. I was about to say something, but– "

"What the hell?" Jack was completely lost. "Parsons said she accidentally put my stuff in the washing machine!"

"Seriously, Jack, do you want me to tell you what happened, or do you just want to keep butting in?"

"Sorry," he muttered, reluctantly. "Go on."

"Thank you. Like I said, at first I just figured she was robbing you, but then she called the sheriff on her radio and he came waddling across the parking lot like he was trying to break the land speed record, all excited, face red as a beetroot. They both looked like they'd found a winning lottery ticket in your pocket." Cathy tapped her ash to the ground. "That's when I hid under the truck. I wanted to see what the hell was going on."

Jack still couldn't see how any of this made a lick of sense. Why would anyone get excited about the contents of his pockets? His phone was just a cheap Android, and there was nothing in his wallet but a few hundred bucks and a couple of credit cards. Not a bad haul for a pickpocket, but it was hardly life changing.

Cathy noticed Jack's confused expression, and finally she enlightened him.

"It was your ID," she said, watching as the light dawned in Jack's eyes. "I'm guessing it says you're a doctor, right?"

Jack nodded. "Yeah, I still have my hospital ID from Saint Francis. I guess I couldn't bring myself to toss it out after I lost my license. You mean they're getting all bent out of shape because I'm a doctor?"

Cathy nodded. "Yeah, and do you know why?"

Jack frowned. "Well, I guess maybe they have some sick—"

"I'm gonna stop you right there, Jack," Cathy interrupted. "You'll never guess in a million years."

She jabbed a finger at the town below. "Plumas Creek isn't just a random little village up in the hills. Do you want to know what it *is*?"

Jack scowled, frustrated and impatient. "Of course I do. Stop screwing around and tell me what's going on."

"They're getting all bent out of shape because it's a damned *survivalist* compound, Jack."

Jack stared at her uncomprehendingly. "A what? Survivalist? Please don't tell me we've wandered into some kind of weird cult thing."

Cathy shook her head. "*No*, it's not a cult thing. Didn't you ever see those shows on TV? Doomsday Preppers? Ringing any bells?"

"No, My wife kept the TV when I moved out," Jack replied. "I just watch whatever sports are playing above the bar."

Cathy sighed, amazed that Jack wasn't familiar. "Survivalists. Preppers. These are folks who believe the end of the world is coming. They think the shit will hit the fan in the form of natural disasters, climate change, outbreaks of disease or, drum roll, please..." she pointed to the sky above her, "nuclear war. They think the government won't be able to handle whatever's coming our way, and when disaster hits it'll take civilized society with it."

Jack raised an eyebrow. "Yeah, I heard about those guys on talk radio. Sounds an awful lot like a cult to me."

"It sounds an awful lot like they're smarter than the rest of us, Jack. A lot of these people have spent years preparing for the collapse. They stockpile food, medicine and clean water. They take themselves off the grid so they'll still have power when the rest of us are freezing our asses off in the dark, and some of them arm themselves so heavily they could outgun a small country. They want to be ready for *anything*."

"This still sounds like it's ticking all the cult boxes. Armed crazy people preparing for the apocalypse? Seems pretty cultish to me."

"Damn it, it's not a cult!" Kathy insisted, lowering her voice when she realized it might carry down the hill. "It's not a cult, Jack. I have a few prepper friends up in Pine Bluff. They're not crazy. Most of them are just regular people who want to be sure they'll get by if anything bad happens. Y'know, like *exactly* this situation we're in right now. It's just common sense to prepare for the worst when you live in a country that has a run on bottled water whenever the weatherman announces a light shower."

"You're telling me these are regular people," Jack argued, "and at the same time you're saying they want to hold me hostage because I'm a doctor? How does that make any sense?"

Cathy looked down at the motel below, narrowing her eyes with loathing. "Oh no, I'm just saying that *most* preppers are regular people. *These* assholes are crazy."

"*Then what the hell are we arguing about?*" Jack hissed.

"Nothing," muttered Cathy. "I just don't want you to paint them all with the same brush. Some of my friends are preppers, but they'd never do anything like this."

"And what is *this*, exactly? I still have no idea what they want with me."

Cathy stubbed out her cigarette on the ground and looked back at Jack. "All I know is what I picked up from the sheriff and his wife, but as far as I understood it they're pretty much all set to survive up here for years without any help. Food, fresh water, solar power, the works. They've been hoarding medicine for years, and they've got a little clinic set up in the church, but it looks like they're missing a doctor."

Jack shook his head in disbelief. "That seems like a pretty massive oversight from people who call themselves preppers."

"No, they *had* a doctor. I might have misunderstood, but they were talking about some guy named Ed Irwin. Apparently he's the local doc and his wife is some kind of nurse, but they're both in Florida for their son's wedding. Sounds like it's just really bad timing, but I'm guessing it'd be a hell of a job to make it all the way across the country right now. They're short a doctor the day the world goes to hell, and then out of the clear blue sky you fall right into their lap."

"So, what? They're planning to hobble me or something? Chain me to a radiator? What's their game plan here?"

Cathy shrugged. "The sheriff and his wife had a pretty huge row about that when they found out who you were. It looked to me like they couldn't agree what to do. Things got pretty damned heated, and then the sheriff stormed over and started screwing with my truck. I figure he was just trying to buy himself some time so he could work out some way of keeping you here permanently."

"But why would they need to screw with the

truck? Why stop us leaving at all? If they need a doctor, why not just ask? It's not like I'd refuse to help."

"You'd help *now*, yeah, but Parsons heard you last night, remember? You told him you were on the way to find your wife and kid. He knows you're out of here as soon as we get gas, and he needs you here for keeps."

"But *why?* Why in God's name would they need to hold a doctor hostage?"

Cathy shot Jack a look that suggested she thought he was simple. "Seriously? Why *wouldn't* they? I don't know what the hell's going on out there, but it seems to me the world's coming to an end. We've got nukes – actual God damned *nukes* – blowing up our cities. This isn't the kind of thing we just shake off. This is it. Game over."

She shook her head. "The way I see it this is survival of the fittest right now, and if a doctor shows up on your doorstep you don't just let him gas up and send him on his way. Hell, I don't even really *blame* them. I can at least understand why they'd want to keep you here."

"*You understand?*" Jack spat the words. "You understand why they'd stop me leaving to save my family?"

"Hey, I said it's survival of the fittest, not survival of the nicest," Cathy shrugged. "And I understand, but I still want to kick their asses. These guys aren't screwing around. I waited about a half hour after the sheriff went back to his house before I climbed out from under the truck, but he must have been sitting out on his porch. Soon as he saw me he must have figured I knew what was going down, and the bastard pulled his gun."

"*Jesus!*" Jack exclaimed, eyes wide. "Do you really think he would have shot you?"

Cathy shrugged. "I didn't stick around long enough to find out. The second I saw him I booked it down the street, then I circled around the gas station and made my way up here as soon as I was sure he wasn't on my tail."

She played nervously with the lighter in her hand, staring down at the parking lot below. "Honestly, though? I think the only reason he didn't shoot me in the back is because he didn't want to wake you up and tip you off."

She tucked the lighter in her pocket and pushed herself from the ground, stretching her aching joints. "Anyway, whether or not he'd actually have pulled the trigger, I don't want to stick around another second. We need to get the hell out before someone does something stupid and one of us ends up dead."

"Agreed," Jack nodded. "We need to find ourselves a new vehicle. The only thing I've seen around here is the sheriff's cruiser, so I guess we should head towards those houses over there." He pointed south towards the cluster of homes by the church. "I can see a couple cars in the driveways from here. I'm guessing most of the town is still at the meeting, so maybe we can break in and grab some keys without sounding the alarm."

Cathy shook her head. "Well, hold up there. I don't want to give up on the truck just yet. I couldn't see what Parsons was doing to it, but I know he was standing on the left side of the engine bay. If I had to guess I'd say he was screwing with the fuses. He'd only have to switch out a couple into the wrong circuits to kill the starter, and it'd be hard to figure out the problem without the fuse box diagram."

"OK, then," Jack nodded. "You know where the diagram is?"

Cathy tapped her head. "Right up here. I've been working on that truck since I was sixteen. I know where everything goes. If we can just get down there without being seen I'm pretty sure I can get it moving." She narrowed her eyes and pointed down to the parking lot. "The only problem is *her*."

Down by the blue house Mrs. Parsons had returned to the kitchen. Jack guessed it was her job to keep tabs on Doug. Gabriela, though, was still lurking over by the picket fence in the yard, keeping watch over the motel. She had her radio clipped to her belt, and Jack knew that if she saw them skulking around the truck it would be game over. He didn't want to find out what Parsons would do if he felt his hand was forced.

"How much time do you need to get the truck running?" he asked.

"If it's just the fuses? Couple of minutes, tops. I have spares in the glove compartment. What are you thinking?"

Jack pushed himself from the ground, brushed the pine needles from his trousers and grabbed Cathy's gun from the ground. "I'm thinking I go back and eat some more pancakes," he said, tucking the gun into the back of his pants and covering it with the tails of his shirt.

"Are you *crazy?*" Cathy stared at him in disbelief. "You want to go back in there?"

"No, not even a little bit, but right now as far as they know I have no idea anything's wrong, and I'm guessing they'll want to keep up the illusion as long as they can. I can use that to buy you some time."

Jack had already started clumsily down the hill. Cathy came chasing after, grabbing his arm.

"Seriously, Jack, this is a really bad idea. Forget the truck. We can just do like you said and head over to the houses. It's much less risky."

Jack shook his head and pulled his arm from Cathy's grasp. "It's not about the truck," he said, speeding his pace down the hill. "I'm not leaving a friend behind."

Cathy tried to pull him back again, but Jack shrugged her away. "Damn it, Jack! Doug's a grown man, and they don't have any reason to hurt him. It's not worth risking your life to save him."

"Doug?" Jack paused and looked back at her. "Sure, I'll get him too, but I was talking about Boomer."

•▼•

CHAPTER TWENTY ONE
HEAT HAZE

A WAVE OF impotent fury crashed over Karen as she watched the Prius tear away from the bus, and it only grew stronger when she noticed that all three of the passengers sitting beside the bus just a moment ago had fled.

She couldn't believe it. They'd weighed up their chance of making it to the safe zone in the bus, and all three of them had decided their odds would be better if they screwed over the people who stopped to help. Not a single one had a scrap of decency..

Valerie ran to join Karen, and as she saw the car shrink into the distance she hurled the jump leads in their direction and screamed at the top of her voice.

"I hope you burn in Hell, you God damned parasites!"

Emily stirred in Karen's arms, opening her eyes with a squinting frown. "Why's everyone shouting, mommy?"

"It's OK, pumpkin," Karen assured her, setting her down in the shade of the bus. "You wait here a second. I just need to have a quick talk with Doctor Ramos and this nice lady."

Emily looked up at Valerie, hurling an unbroken stream of expletives at the cloud of dust vanishing into the distance, then she looked back at her mom with a doubtful expression.

"Well, I'm sure she's usually nice. Hang on a minute." Karen hurried over to Valerie and whispered in her ear, and with a start Valerie turned to the little girl who'd just soaked up a dozen new curse words like a sponge.

"I'm so sorry, darling," Valerie said, breathing heavily, trying to bring her anger under control, but she was almost vibrating with fury. She stalked back to the bus and kicked its side with a cry of *"God damn it!"*

Emily flinched at the sound of clanging steel, her lower lip wobbling as tears threatened to burst forth.

"OK," Ramos said calmly, taking on the role of peacemaker, "I don't think we're going to achieve anything by kicking everything in sight. Val, is there any chance we could push start this thing?"

Valerie kicked at the dirt, her fists clenched. "No! We already tried it. Damn thing weighs about thirteen tons, so unless you have Captain America hiding behind you it's not moving an inch."

"And there's no way to, I don't know, jump start it without another battery?"

Valerie shot Ramos a withering look.

"I'm guessing that's a no. OK then, it looks like we have to do this on foot."

"On foot?" Karen asked doubtfully, looking up at the cloudless sky. "Looks like it's gonna be a hot day, Doc. How far do you think we could make it? Val, do you have any water on the bus?"

"No, there's nothing left," Valerie replied. "They only had enough for one bottle per passenger the last place we stopped, and those ungrateful pricks drank it all hours ago."

"And do you have any clue where we are? We passed a little town about… what was it, Doc, maybe ten miles back? You think we could make it that far?"

Valerie shook her head, and without another word

she climbed back into the bus and went straight for the driver's seat.

"Hang on," she called down. "The army guys at Vallejo were handing out maps to the safe zone." Empty styrofoam cups and candy wrappers fell to the ground as Valerie pick through the mess of her seat, and eventually she came up a single sheet of paper.

"Here we go," she said, emerging from the bus brandishing the map. She dropped to her haunches in the shade and set it down on the asphalt. "OK, we've been sticking to the smaller roads, but I know we crossed route 65 not so far back. That's the little town you saw. I think it was called…" she traced a finger down the map. "*There.* That was Wheatland. It looked abandoned to me, so I'm not sure heading in that direction would do us much good, but look at this." She ran her finger along the county route until it hit a grayed out patch.

"This is Beale Air Force Base. I saw signs for it a few miles back. Can't be more than five miles in that direction."

Karen followed her finger, pointed ahead down the narrow, dusty road. In that direction she could see nothing but empty fields all the way to the horizon. There wasn't a single building anywhere in sight. She sighed.

"Then I guess we have no choice. It's either head for the base or stay here and die of thirst. What do you think, Doc?"

Ramos gave her a joyless smile. "Well, I'm a fan of water, to be honest. Never go a day without it, and I'm guessing the base has faucets."

Karen nodded. "I'd think so, yeah. And maybe some food. That's settled, then. Emily, honey, we're going to go for a little walk."

Emily sat with her back against the bus, her lip still quivering, and she leaned in towards Karen and whispered. "Not with the angry lady. I don't want to go with her."

"I'm sorry, pumpkin, but we have to all go together. We need to go get some water, and the angry lady needs some too, OK?" Karen turned to Valerie and gave her a reassuring smile. "No offense. We've met some pretty unpleasant people on the road. I guess she's having some trust issues."

Valerie shuffled in towards Emily, who backed away a little as she approached. "Hey, Emily," she said, her voice soft and quiet. "I'm sorry if I scared you a little. I didn't mean to yell. I'm not really a mean lady, I just got a little mad for a while." She reached to her collar and tugged loose her bright red neck tie. "I'll tell you what. If you let me come with you I'll let you have this. Isn't it pretty? What do you say?"

Emily looked at Karen and then back to Valerie, nodding uncertainly as Valerie draped it over her neck. "Oh my, that looks beautiful. You want to go for a walk now?"

Emily sniffed, then took Valerie's outstretched hand and lifted herself from the ground.

"Do you like to ride the bus, Emily? Maybe when we get back home I could take you and your mom on a tour. You can have the whole wide bus all to yourself. What do you think about that?"

Emily nodded again, then looked back towards Karen. "Mommy, can we?"

Karen smiled. "Sure we can, honey, if Valerie says it's OK."

Emily grinned up at Valerie, her fear forgotten. "Mommy says we can!"

"Well that's *great!* Hey, should we invite the doctor as well?"

"Yeah, he can come too," Emily laughed, wiping her nose with the back of her hand. "He's OK, I guess."

"Yeah, I think so too." Valerie started walking, and Emily followed beside her hand in hand. "Now, I want to hear *aaaallll* about you. Do you have a favorite teacher at school?"

Karen and Ramos followed ten steps behind as Emily launched into an enthusiastic story about Miss Jessop and her music class, and for a long while Karen just let her daughter's voice wash over her as she walked. It was nice to forget for a moment about all that had happened. To forget the fact that the world behind them, the life they'd always known, sat in a pile of rubble and ash.

It was nice to just listen to Emily talk about normal life. The pictures she'd drawn in art class. The monkeys she'd seen when her dad took her to the zoo. The dog that lived next door, covered in white fur apart from two circles of black around its eyes that made it look like she was wearing glasses.

For a mile or so Karen let herself believe that when all this was over they could go back to that life. Back to the little house in the suburbs. Back to the school and Miss Jessop's art class. Back to the cute little bespectacled dog. She didn't have the energy to face up to the future just yet, and listening to Emily felt as relaxing as lowering herself into a hot bubble bath.

The bus was a dot behind them by the time Emily finally talked herself out, and in the silence Ramos finally gave an awkward cough.

"Listen," he said, looking down at his feet. "I'm sorry for telling you to turn around. I guess we should have just kept on driving, huh?"

Karen took a moment to consider her reply. She could easily lay into him for the decision that led them to lose the car. She knew he wouldn't punch back. She knew she could take out all her frustrations on him, whether or not it was fair, but eventually she shook her head.

"Don't beat yourself up about it, Doc. You were right. We needed to do a good deed, and we did it. Yeah, we got burned, but I guess that's a chance you have to take."

She took a deep breath, looking ahead at Emily holding hands with Valerie. "If we're going to go into the future every man for himself I don't know if we deserve to survive, know what I mean? I don't want Emily to have to grow up in a world where people don't help each other." She fell silent for a moment, and then a slight smile played across her lips. "Besides, it's not all bad. Looks like you got to be the knight in shining armor."

She turned to Ramos and noticed him blushing. He was looking ahead to Valerie. "So, she knows exactly which days you ride the bus, huh? That's… oddly specific. You think she does that for all her passengers?"

Ramos' cheeks were burning now. He looked down at his feet with an embarrassed smile.

"And you bake cookies for all your bus drivers?" She grinned, enjoying Ramos' awkward silence, then leaned in and whispered in a sing song tone. "Cesar and Valerie, sittin' in a tree, K.I.S– "

"OK, wise ass, that's quite enough of that."

"Oh come on, Doc, it's not every day I get to see a beautiful love story play out against the stark backdrop of a nuclear holocaust. I'm guessing Hollywood has been flattened, so I have to take my entertainment where I can get it. So, you planning to ask her out? I bet she'd– "

"Hang on," Ramos interrupted, peering out at the road ahead. "Do you see that?"

Karen followed his gaze towards the horizon, but she couldn't see anything but the shimmering heat haze that made it look like the road ran straight into a lake about a mile up ahead. "What? What am I looking at?"

Ramos frowned and squinted. "It's hard to see, but... doesn't that look like a car to you?"

Karen looked again, squinting as if the rippling heat haze might lift if only she could focus hard enough. She couldn't be sure, but there *did* seem to be something on the road ahead, a shimmering dark dot that seemed to drift in and out of sight.

"I see something, I think, but I couldn't say if it was a car. Could just be a tree."

"No," Ramos shook his head, still staring. "No, that's no tree." He picked up his pace to catch up with Valerie, and Karen hurried after him. "Hey guys," he said, taking Valerie by the shoulder, "you might want to drop back behind me. I think there's a car up ahead."

Karen smiled as Ramos forged on ahead, taking the lead in a transparent attempt to impress Valerie. Even if it *was* a car she couldn't imagine it being any sort of threat to them, but she decided to play the role of wingwoman for a minute.

"Hold up a minute, Emily," she said, taking her daughter by the hand. "Doctor Ramos is going on ahead to make sure it's safe for us."

Karen didn't want to voice her hope for fear that she might jinx it, but a little part of her believed that the guys who stole the Prius might have had a sudden attack of conscience. Maybe they'd realized after a mile or so that stranding people by the side of the road was a crappy thing to do. Maybe, just *maybe*, they were thinking about turning back to pick them up.

She kept her fingers crossed as she followed a few dozen yards behind Ramos, striding ahead with purpose, and Karen couldn't help but notice that his show of bravado seemed to be working. Valerie looked to be impressed by the Doc taking the lead.

Through the haze up ahead the shimmering dot became a shape, and it wasn't long before Karen realized it really *was* a car. It didn't seem to be moving, though. From this distance it looked like it was stopped by the side of the road, and after a few dozen more steps Karen began to feel a touch of apprehension.

"Hey, Doc?" she called ahead. "That's our Prius, right?"

Ramos began to slow. Unless there just happened to be another silver Prius on this isolated country road it was theirs, but even from a hundred yards away it was clear it wasn't just parked. The car was half off the road on the dusty verge, stopped at an angle as if it had come to a sudden, screeching halt.

"Stay back, girls," Ramos called out. "I'm gonna go... umm, check it out."

It looked as if the Doc's desire to impress Valerie was coming up against his fear, and the bravado was only just winning out. He moved forward at a slow shuffle, as if the Prius might rear up and attack at any moment. He approached the car cautiously, moving in a wide arc around the side, and when he finally came within a dozen steps of it he suddenly stopped.

"Oh, God!" he gasped, turning back to the women and waving them away. "Stay there!"

"What is it?" Karen called out, her voiced edged with tension. "What's wrong?"

Ramos didn't answer. He just held out a staying hand and began to approach the car, even more cautiously now.

"Cesar, what is it?" demanded Valerie.

Ramos drew level with the car now, hunched down and ready to run if something happened. He reached out to the driver's door, but thought better of pulling the handle.

"They're dead," he called out, taking a step back. "They're all dead."

Karen grabbed Emily by the hand and held it tight

as Valerie hurried towards the car, and when she reached it she stopped short and held her hand to her mouth. "Oh my God," she gasped, staring at what was left of the Prius.

Karen approached now, driven forward by morbid curiosity. These guys had been alive just a half hour ago, and despite her fear she needed to know what had happened to them. She came as close as she dared, holding Emily in place behind her so she was shielded from the sight, and she gasped as she saw what remained of the car.

The front windshield was completely shattered. Bullet holes peppered the hood, and the front tires were flat. Inside the car the driver and passengers were…

She turned away, sickened by the sight.

"Who could have done this?" Valerie asked, tears in her eyes.

A few dozen steps behind them Karen lifted Emily from the ground and turned her away from the car, carefully shielding her from the sight as she approached. "Don't look, honey," she warned, skirting around the wrecked Prius as far away as possible. She scanned the road ahead and the farmland that surrounded them, searching for movement, but there was nothing. There wasn't even a breeze to trouble the crops. Wherever the attackers had come from they hadn't stuck around for long.

"What is it, mommy?" Emily pestered, trying to sneak a look at the car.

Karen held her daughter's head against her shoulder, pulling her a little too tight, but she didn't want this image burned into Emily's memory. "It's nothing, honey, just don't look. Doc, what are you doing?" she demanded, her voice shrill with fear.

Ramos had taken another step towards the car, and very slowly he reached out and opened the driver's door. The driver was slumped against it, and as the door swung open his body began to fall out.

"Doc! Leave it alone!"

"Mommy, what's he doing?" Emily tried to turn her head, but Karen just held on tighter.

Ramos lifted the driver's body back into the seat like a sack of potatoes, keeping his hands clear of the blood plastered across the front of his shirt from several chest wounds.

"Hang on, I just need to…" He leaned across the driver, stretching to reach something tucked into a cubby between the front seats, but just as his fingers got a grip on it he lurched, jumping so high that his head hit the ceiling of the car, and he scrambled backwards and fell on his ass in the middle of the road.

"Oh, Jesus Christ, I thought he was still alive!" he gasped, his face pink. "I thought I heard him breathe!"

Karen clamped her free hand over Emily's ear, pulled her head against her chest and angrily hissed. "What the *hell* do you think you're doing, Doc? You're scaring us!"

Ramos wiped a sheen of sweat from his forehead and pushed himself back to his feet. "Sorry, sorry, he's dead. I just…" He held up a plastic grocery bag. "You need your medicine."

Karen felt her anger seeping away. "Well… thanks," she reluctantly conceded. "But can we please get out of here now? I want to get off this damned road before that happens to us."

Before Karen had finished speaking she realized it was already too late. Valerie's hand shot out, pointing towards a column of dust rising from the road a half mile ahead. Beneath it another black dot shimmered in the haze, but there was no mistaking this one for a tree.

"Oh God," Valerie cried, turning to Ramos with

wide, terrified eyes. *"They're coming back!"*

Karen could hear the engine now, a threatening roar that grew louder by the second, and she watched in horror as the dot resolved into the shape of a truck.

"We have to get off the road, *now!*"

Without waiting to see if the others were following Karen ran north into the flat, featureless fields that seemed to stretch all the way to the horizon. She knew there was nowhere to hide. There wasn't so much as a tree in sight, nor even any tall crops to hide amongst, but there was no time to worry about where she was going. As the truck bore down on the Prius she knew the only important thing was to get *away*, as far as possible. If they could only make it far enough across the fields that it was too much effort for the attackers to follow they might just…

But no. Karen risked a glance behind her, and her heart sank. Ramos and Valerie were following just a few steps behind, but behind *them* the truck had reached the Prius, and with a feeling of utter dread Karen watched as it turned off the road and pursued them into the field.

She tried to run faster, but she was struggling under Emily's weight. Beneath her feet the field was uneven and furrowed, pockmarked with small burrows that threatened to swallow her feet, and it wasn't long before one of them caught her. She tripped, turning her ankle on some invisible obstacle, tumbling sideways to protect Emily from the shock of the ground.

Now she could hear the engine growing louder. She tried to stand, but her foot was bound up in something, a length of thin wire that seemed to run the length of the field almost hidden beneath the grass. She kicked it off, freeing herself, but she knew it was already too late. The truck was too close, looming over them. There was no way they could escape.

She rolled on top of Emily as the hiss of air brakes told her the truck had arrived. She pulled her daughter close and held her tight, trying to block out the world, whispering a prayer that whatever was about to happen it would at least be quick.

She heard yelling. Sharp, quick shouts. Orders.

Her mind was buzzing with terror, and as she looked up she couldn't make out what they were saying. Everyone seemed to be yelling at once. She saw uniforms. Saw their lips move. She saw Ramos and Valerie drop to their knees and clasp their hands behind their heads. She saw a man stand over her, the sunlight casting a bright halo around him. A rifle pointed at her face as she squinted up at him.

"What do you want?" she cried, her eyes welling with tears. *"I don't understand!"*

Another two men pushed past the man aiming the rifle. One of them took hold of Emily, dragging her away by her arms, and Karen screamed with a terrified rage. She tried to launch herself at the man, to grab Emily back and hold her close, but before she'd even made it to her feet she saw the butt of a rifle headed for her face.

Everything went blank as she tumbled back to the ground. Her ears rang and her vision swam. She felt someone haul her to her knees. They grabbed her hands and pulled them roughly behind her back. She felt the bite of plastic strip ties bind her wrists, and then finally the ringing in her ears began to fade.

And then the voices found their way past her terror, and suddenly it all became clear.

"You are trespassing on United States Air Force property. You're all under arrest."

•▼•

CHAPTER TWENTY TWO
WE'VE GOT COMPANY

JACK NERVOUSLY ROUNDED the corner of the motel, approaching from the street in the direction of the gas station, trying to make it seem as if he'd just been on a stroll around town. It had taken him twenty minutes to work his way across the steep slope and make it around the station, but he figured Gabriela would be less suspicious if she saw him returning from the street than stumbling out from the pine forest.

His throat was dry and his heart pounded as he saw her waiting in the yard of the Parsons house. He walked as casually as he could, but he'd never been any good at acting. He was excruciatingly aware of his every movement. He felt like a kid in his first school play, awkwardly walking on stage and freezing in the lights.

"*Hola*," Gabriela waved, smiling just as casually as Jack walked, but now he was looking for it Jack could see the sharp edges of her smile. There was no warmth there. Beneath her friendly mask she was surveying him, wondering where he'd been, looking for a hint that he might know something was amiss. "You went for a walk?"

Jack patted his stomach and flashed a weak smile. "Just a quick mile up the street and back. I needed to settle my stomach. Not feeling too great this morning."

Gabriela's smile faltered for a moment, but she quickly recovered. "Mrs. Parsons is waiting for you in the kitchen. You can go in."

"Thanks, I'll just… Yeah, thanks." Jack glanced over towards the truck. At this angle Gabriela would easily see Cathy when she tried to approach. On either side of the truck there were at least ten yards of open ground to cover, and she'd need to pop the hood to get to the fuse box. He needed to get the maid out of the way.

"Hey," he said, stepping over the fence into the

yard, "I don't suppose you have any antacid, do you?" He could almost hear the final nail being hammered into the coffin of his James Bond fantasy. He pulled a sour face and held his stomach, as if he were in pain. "I don't think that breakfast agreed with me."

Gabriela shook her head, turning away from the parking lot to face him. "I'm sorry, I don't have any." She pointed towards the house. "Maybe you could ask Mrs. Parsons if she has something."

"OK, thanks, I guess I'll…" Jack fell silent and began to blow out his cheeks, swallowing as if he was trying to hold back vomit. "Oh, God."

Gabriela's expression turned to concern. "Are you OK?"

He shook his head, suddenly rushing across the lawn to the side of the house, where he doubled over and planted his hands against the wall. "I think I'm gonna…" He let out a pained gasp and heaved his shoulders. Behind him he heard Gabriela rush to his side, and as he looked behind him from his bent double stance he saw, upside down, Cathy rushing across the parking lot towards the truck.

Time to take one for the team, Jack. He hated vomiting with a passion, but he knew he had to make this convincing, so with a sharp convulsion of his diaphragm he squeezed his stomach, strained his throat and puked at the foot of the wall, almost choking with the effort.

"Oh God, I'm so sorry," he gasped. "I'm so embarrassed." He spat the bitter taste from his mouth. "Could you... could you please get me a glass of water?" he gasped, still gagging. "I... I think I'll feel better once I've had a little water."

Gabriela rubbed him on the back. "Yes, of course. Water is good. Mrs. Parsons can get you some in the kitchen."

Jack turned to face her, letting an ugly gob of drool fall from his lips. "Would you mind getting it for me? I... I mean, I don't want to go indoors and vomit all over the floor. I'll wait just outside."

Without waiting for an answer he pushed off the wall and took hold of Gabriela's arm, pushing her towards the back of the house as if she was leading him there.

"God bless you," he said, drool still hanging from his lips. "I don't know what's come over me. I don't usually get sick like this. I'm so sorry you had to see that. I'll clean it up, I promise."

"It's OK, don't worry," Gabriela assured him, struggling as Jack laid his weight against her. "Come on, we're almost there. Mrs. Parsons!" she called out. "Mrs. Parsons, could you help us?"

Jack sped his pace, realizing that if the sheriff's wife came outside she might see Cathy. "It's alright!" he yelled, staggering towards the kitchen door. "I'm… I'm alright."

Mrs. Parsons appeared at the door just as Jack reached it, and he barreled into her with enough force to send her reeling back into the kitchen. "I'm sorry!" he blurted out, still clutching Gabriela's arm. "I just need a glass of water."

"Good Lord, Jack, are you quite alright?" On the far side of the kitchen table Garside pushed back his chair and rushed towards him. "What's wrong?"

Jack released Gabriela's arm and took two staggering steps away from her. "I'll be OK, Doug, I'm just feeling a little woozy," he said. "Oh, here it comes again." He swooned forward, knocking aside a dining chair and clutching at Garside's tweed jacket as if he couldn't stay standing without it. He leaned against his shoulder and turned his head.

"*Get Boomer,*" he whispered urgently in Garside's ear. "*We need to get out of here now!*"

As he staggered back a step he could tell from Garside's expression that he wasn't quick on the uptake. "What was that, old chap?" he asked, his face plastered in a guileless smile. "I didn't quite catch what you said."

"Here you go, Jack," Mrs. Parsons said, scurrying over with a glass of water cradled in her hands. "You'll feel better after this. My, I hope it wasn't something I served that disagreed with you."

Jack shook his head as he gulped the water. "No," he said, gasping over the rim of the glass. "Don't worry, this is something I've had for a while," he lied. "I just need my medication. It's still in your suitcase out in the truck, right, Doug?"

Jack put everything he had into the look he shot at Garside. The wide eyed *just agree with me* glare would have won him awards in a just world, but Garside's face was a mask of blank incomprehension.

"You put something in my case?"

"Yeah, remember?" Jack squeezed Doug's arm as tight as he dared, not quite enough to make him squeal in pain but enough, hopefully, to finally get the message across. "Back in Pine Bluff. I put it in there when we switched cars, but I don't know the combination to the lock. Can you open it for me? It's in the back of the truck."

"Lock?" Garside frowned. "On *my* suitcase?" For a

moment it looked as if the message had once again sailed a mile over Garside's head, but finally, after an excruciating silence, a faint glimmer of light dawned in his eyes.

"Oh, *that* suitcase! Sorry, I thought you were talking about the other one. Yes, yes, of course, I remember seeing your medicine in there. You want me to get it now?"

"Yeah, I should take it before I hurl again." Jack breathed a sigh of relief as Garside took his arm and led him back towards the door, only for Mrs. Parsons to try to block their way.

"Why don't you take a seat, Jack?" she asked, nodding to the table with an expression of concern. "I'm sure Douglas can fetch your medicine for you." She pulled back a chair. "Go on, rest your legs. I'll get you some more water."

Jack pushed past her, noting the slightly panicked look in her eyes. It was clear she was afraid of letting him leave. "Thank you, Mrs. Parsons, but– "

"Joan, please. Come on, you look like death. Take a seat."

"Thank you, no. I'll be right back once I've taken my pills. Come on, Boomer."

He continued out the door, relieved to see that the

dog had for once decided to obey a command, trotting out ahead of him into the yard. Mrs. Parsons followed them out, trailing Gabriela behind her, and she seemed to grow more agitated with each step Jack and Garside took towards the parking lot.

"I can get you some juice if you'd prefer," she offered, trying to tempt him back inside, "or I could even make up some lemonade in the SodaStream!"

Jack ignored her, pushing on through the yard and stepping over the fence. She didn't sound like she was willing to try to stop them by force, but he kept a hand free in case he had to reach for the gun tucked in his waistband.

On the other side of the parking lot he saw a flash of movement, and his heart skipped a beat as he saw Cathy duck down in the driver's seat of the truck. A moment later the engine roared to life, and Jack broke into a shambling half jog as Cathy threw the Ford into reverse and steered towards them.

"*Please!*" The panic in Mrs. Parsons voice was undisguised now. "*Please don't go!*"

Jack looked back as he grabbed the handle and yanked open the back door, pushing Garside and Boomer into the truck ahead of him. By the picket fence Mrs. Parsons stood, red faced and on the verge of tears, wringing her hands with worry as she watched Jack climb into the truck.

"*He'll hurt you if you try to leave!*" she yelled.

Jack slammed the door behind him without a response, and as soon as she saw that everyone was aboard Cathy shoved the truck back into drive, powered it out of the parking lot and swept out onto the road. Through the rear windshield Jack could see Gabriela talking on her radio as Mrs. Parsons wept with frustration, and he felt his heart begin to race. It was obvious the maid was warning the sheriff of their departure.

He just hoped Parsons wouldn't try anything stupid.

"How are we doing for gas, Cathy?" Jack demanded, leaning over the back seat.

Cathy frowned at the gauge. The needle hovered just inside the red zone. "Well, it didn't magically multiply while we were parked last night, if that's what you're asking, so it's touch and go whether we'll make it to the next gas station. Let's just keep our fingers and toes crossed."

"And let's hope the owner of the station isn't a friend of Parsons," said Jack. "I'd hate to have to– "

"I'm sorry," Garside angrily interjected, "but is

nobody going to explain to me what in blazes we're doing? Jack, what was all that palaver about medicine back there? And you, miss," he said, poking a finger at Cathy, "I thought you'd scarpered last night. What the bloody hell is going on here?"

Cathy stepped on the gas as the truck roared out of town and the forest enclosed them once again. "You'll have to wait until we're a long way from here for the long version, Doug, but the quick and dirty of it is that there were some bad folks back there. Parsons wants to hold Jack hostage because he's a doctor. We're pretty much expendable, and the sheriff probably isn't totally against the idea of killing us to keep the Doc in town."

Garside sat back primly in his seat, straightening out the creases in his jacket. "Right then," he said, his face turning a sickly shade, "well I suppose we'd better push on, then, hadn't we?" He turned to look out the window, frowning at the forest whipping by, and after a long, contemplative silence he muttered to himself, "You know, *I* wanted to go to Mallorca, but *no*, we have to go to America, she says. It'll be so bloody romantic. We'll see the– "

"Quiet, Doug," Jack hissed, craning over his shoulder to look out the rear windshield. He punched his fist against the back of his seat, swearing under his breath. "Cathy, can this thing go any faster?"

Cathy pressed her foot to the floor, and with a whine of protest from the engine the truck lurched forward. "A little, but we're really burning through gas here. Why, do you see something?"

Jack nodded, grimacing. "Yeah, looks like we've got company."

•▼•

CHAPTER TWENTY THREE
HOLD STILL NOW

"COMPANY?" GARSIDE TWISTED in his seat. "What do you mean, company?"

Following behind the truck, visible only when the road straightened out, Sheriff Parsons' police cruiser raced towards them, closely followed by a rusting beige pickup that eagerly jostled for position. Every time the cars came into view they seemed to have closed the gap a little more, edging nearer whenever the road allowed for a burst of acceleration.

Jack knew that it was only a matter of time before they caught up. There was no escaping them. There was only one road, penned in by thick forest on either side, and even if the truck made it all the way to the turnoff they'd missed the night before Jack knew they had no other option but to take it. There were no gas stations back in the direction they'd approached the town. Their only hope was to reach the station in Greenville.

What's more, Parsons knew it too. He knew time was on his side. He only had to wait until their tank ran dry, and when they finally rolled to a halt they'd be sitting ducks, entirely at his mercy.

Jack narrowed his eyes, glaring at the cruiser, praying for it to collide with the pickup and spin off into the forest. He knew that only a crash or a breakdown would prevent it from catching them. Eventually he sighed, coming to a decision.

"Cathy, pull over," he said, glowering back at the approaching cars.

"Pull over? *Are you crazy?*"

"Just… just pull over, OK? Please. We have to have this out right now." He reached to the small of his back and drew out Cathy's pistol. "There's no point in dragging it out."

Cathy scowled at him in the rear view, but she reluctantly slowed the truck and pulled in to the side of the road. "Have it your way," she sighed. "But please tell me you at least have some kind of a plan."

"Plan?" Jack stared down at the pistol in his hands. It had been years since he'd fired any kind of weapon, and he didn't intend to break that streak. He pressed the magazine release, slipped it out and checked it before pushing it firmly back in. Almost full.

"My plan is to try to reason with him," he said, handing the pistol over the driver's seat to Cathy. "Take this. I don't think he's a monster, and I don't think he really wants to hurt anybody. I think he's just dumb and panicked, and if I don't give him the chance to walk away he's going to do something stupid that gets us all killed."

Cathy took the pistol and set it down in the cubby between the seats, and Jack reached beneath the driver's seat and pulled out the gun he'd taken from Warren. He released the magazine and pulled back the slide to double check that it was empty.

Now the cruiser was clearly visible, moving at a crawl a hundred yards behind the truck. Parsons seemed to be sizing up the situation, trying to figure out why they'd stopped.

Jack pushed open the back door, grabbing Boomer by the collar as she tried to rush out between his legs. "Stay here, girl," he said. "This stop isn't for you."

Now Parsons was speaking to the driver of the

pickup beside him, giving instructions, and a moment later the vehicle tore ahead. Jack watched, his every muscle tensed, as the pickup pulled alongside their truck. It parked at an angle just ahead of them, blocking them from a clean getaway.

Through the window Jack recognized the driver. It was the same man who'd knocked on the kitchen door at breakfast. Tall and wiry, with a pitiful attempt at a beard sprouting in patches across his face. *Ray? Roy?* Jack couldn't remember, but he narrowed his eyes as the man glared back at him from the front seat of the pickup.

He took a deep breath, trying to steady his nerves. "If he doesn't back down," he said quietly, "I want you to just get out of here. Don't do anything dumb. Just… just take care of Boomer, OK? Can you grab his collar, Doug?"

Garside reached out and pulled Boomer towards him, his face glowing red with indignation. "Now hold on a minute, chap. You can't just ask us to leave you behind! I'm no action hero, but that's… well, it's just not cricket!"

"He doesn't want *you*, Doug. He wants *me,* and if he needs a doctor badly enough… look, just don't make this the hill you die on." Jack reached out and took Garside's hand. "Thank you, Douglas. I hope you find your wife."

Garside looked like he was fighting back tears, clutching Jack's hand for dear life. He turned to Cathy. "You're not to drive off, understand? We're not leaving him behind!"

"It's OK, Doug," Jack reassured him. "Don't worry about me." He reached forward and squeezed Cathy's shoulder. "Wish me luck."

Before Cathy could reply he pushed himself out of his seat, his shoes crunching in the gravel beside the road, and he pushed the door closed on Boomer as she strained against her collar, trying to follow him out.

As Jack stepped away from the car Sheriff Parsons' cruiser pulled to a stop across the street, and the sheriff hauled himself out from the driver's seat with a groan. He hitched up his pants as he stood, the sunlight catching the grip of the gun in his holster, and he gave Jack an almost apologetic smile.

"I was really hoping we could do this the easy way, Jack," he sighed. "You know we had a brainstorm down at the church this morning, trying to come up with ways to get you to stay? They came up with all sorts of ideas. Y'know, landslides blocking the roads, bad gas pumps... we were even toying with the idea of making a fake radio announcement about fallout to the south." He shook his head and let out a chuckle. "Could have been nice, y'know, if you thought we weren't keeping you here on purpose. Could have all been nice and friendly."

Parsons pushed his door closed with a sense of finality, as if to declare that the time for friendliness had come to an end.

"But then your buddy there had to go and eavesdrop on a conversation that wasn't meant for her, didn't she?" He looked over at Cathy through the side window of the truck, nodding with a cold smile and raising his voice. "Sort of forced our hand, young lady. Forced us into something a little more drastic." He waved over to the pickup truck as the driver climbed out, and pointed to Jack. "Check him, Ray."

Jack locked eyes with the sheriff as Ray approached behind him, and he held still as the man patted him down before pulling the gun from his waistband. "You don't have to do anything, Bill. We can just drive away from here, no harm, no foul. I don't care about whatever you have going on here. Nobody needs to know about this. We can just go our separate ways."

Parsons sighed, tapping a fist gently on the roof of his cruiser as he glumly shook his head. "I wish it were that simple, Jack, I really do, but you know I can't let you leave. I've got a hundred forty seven people here in Plumas Creek, and I promised I'd take care of them. I gave them my *word,* Jack. You understand that kind of responsibility, right?" He let out a snort of air through his nose. "Look who I'm asking. Of course you understand. You've got a daughter."

Jack bristled with anger at the mention of Emily, but he managed to remain silent.

"Now I'm sure you'd be willing to burn the world to the ground to protect your little girl. We got kids here in Plumas Creek, too. Couple dozen of them, and God only knows how long they'll last without a doctor. You understand why I can't put your kid above all of ours, right? That just wouldn't be fair, know what I mean?"

Jack felt his fists clench as he grimaced at the sheriff. He'd love nothing more than to pummel his face until he felt his knuckles hit the back of the man's skull.

"You can't force me to treat your people, sheriff.

You know it can't work like that. You can handcuff me to a patient's bed, but I won't lift a finger to help. Not under duress."

Parsons flashed a cold smile as he used a finger to wipe the sleep from his eye. "Yeah," he sighed, "I figured you'd say something like that. That's what I told Joan this morning. I said this doc, now he's not a man to be messed with. She's got a good heart, my Joan. She thought we should try the softly, softly approach. Y'know, appeal to your better nature, try to bring you onside, but I told her that wouldn't work with a man like you. See, I know people, and I could see as soon as I looked at you you've got a length of rebar running down your spine."

As Parsons had been talking Ray had wandered back to his truck, and now the sheriff nodded to him. "Bring out the girl," he ordered.

"What?" Jack turned to see the man pull open the driver's door of Cathy's truck and take her roughly by the arm. *"No!* Leave her alone!"

The sheriff reached for his holster as Ray dragged Cathy down to the street, and he took a step forward as he pulled his revolver free. "Like I told Joan, if we wanna get to a man like you we have to show we mean business. No half measures. We have to show him what he has to lose before he'll play ball."

Cathy fought back against Ray, trying to pull free of his grip. "*Get your hands off me, you asshole!*"

"Quiet her down, Ray," Parsons said, and as Jack glared at the sheriff with undisguised hatred he heard a sharp slap behind him, and he turned to see Cathy double over in pain.

"Way I see it, Jack, you've got pretty much nothing left. If your wife and kid are still alive they might as well be on the moon, for all the good it'll do you. You ain't getting all the way down to... where was it, Modesto?" He shook his head. "Not a chance. They're gone, understand?" He flipped out the cylinder of the revolver, checking the chambers before flipping it closed with a click. "The way I see things you got nothing left but these folks here, so they'll be... what's the word? Collateral?"

He pondered it for a moment.

"Yeah, that works. They'll be my collateral. Every time you decide you don't want to be a doctor any more I'll put a bullet in one of your buddies. Nothing too serious, you understand. Just a flesh wound, something you can treat with a little antiseptic and a bandage. No painkillers, though. Those are reserved for my people."

Jack watched in horror as Ray shoved Cathy to the ground in front of the sheriff. "So what should we try first, Jack? Arm or leg?"

"Stop!" Jack felt the blood run cold in his veins, his hatred chilling him to his core. "Just... stop. I'll do it. Leave her alone. I'll be your doctor."

Parsons took Cathy by the arm with his free hand, pressing the barrel of the revolver against the fleshiest part of her bicep. "That's nice to hear, Jack. I'm glad you're on board, but you understand I have to show you that I'm not screwing around here. What good's a threat if you're not sure I'll really follow through, know what I mean?"

"Please!" Jack hated himself for giving in. Hated the high pitched squeal of his voice as he pleaded. Hated the pain as he dropped to his knees on the hard asphalt, clasping his hands together. "I believe you! Don't hurt her!"

For what felt like an eternity Parsons held the gun against Cathy's arm, staring at Jack as if sizing him up. As if he was wondering if he'd really broken him, or if Jack was just trying to play him. Parsons squeezed a little on the trigger, and Jack flinched as he watched the hammer draw back.

Time seemed to stop. The hammer hovered half

way back, perfectly balanced, ready to snap forward if Jack breathed wrong. Jack stared at it, unblinking. He'd swear he could see it twitch each time the sheriff's heart beat.

And then it eased forward as Parsons relaxed his grip on the trigger. He pulled the gun from Cathy's arm, and as he released her she fell to the ground in tears, shaking with terror.

"I really want to believe you, Jack," sighed Parsons, ignoring the woman at his feet as he ran a thoughtful hand across his double chin. "I'm half way there. I don't want to have to shoot the girl, but..." He wavered for a moment, moving the barrel of the gun back and forth across Cathy's body, his finger still hovering close to the trigger. "I just can't let you think I'm a soft touch, you know? It wouldn't set the right tone for our relationship."

With a frustrated growl he finally waved the revolver away from Cathy. "OK, I'm gonna let the girl take a rain check for today, as I'm in a good mood. You'd better be thankful Joan fed me a decent breakfast this morning. You should be sure to thank her, otherwise this could have turned out different."

Jack let out the breath he'd been holding since Parsons had touched his finger to the trigger. He felt his heart fluttering in his chest, and the acrid taste of bile burned the back of his throat. He felt like he didn't have the strength to lift himself from the ground, his legs were trembling so much.

And then his heart stopped beating as Parsons turned to Ray and muttered another order.

"Go fetch the dog."

Jack watched as Ray returned to the truck. "No," he muttered, watching the man yank open the back door and grab Boomer by the collar, pulling him away from Garside. He felt as if he had no strength left as Ray walked the dog back towards Parsons. "Please, no. She's just a dog," he pleaded once again.

He felt his bottom lip quiver as Parsons hefted the revolver once again. "The girl gets a pass, Jack, but I still have to prove I'm not all talk." Ray sat Boomer down at the sheriff's feet, and she looked back at Jack with wide eyes, her tongue lolling from her mouth as she panted.

"I want you to remember this, Jack. I want it seared into your memory, understand?" He cocked back the hammer of the revolver. The click as it locked in place seemed deafening against the silence of the forest, and Parsons lowered the gun until the barrel was pressed against the back of Boomer's head.

"Please," Jack wept now, the tears streaming unashamedly down his cheeks. "Please don't do this."

Parsons closed his eyes and shook his head, taking a deep breath. "I want you to know that I don't *want* to do this, Jack. It's important you know that. I'm not Satan. I don't enjoy this, but I have a hundred forty seven people to keep alive. I have to be *sure* you know what happens if you don't play ball, Jack. I have to be *certain*."

Jack took a final look at Boomer, his vision blurred by tears of desperation. His mind willed him to throw himself forward, to tackle Parsons to the ground and beat him to death with his own gun, but his legs just wouldn't listen to his commands. He screamed at them in his head, pleading with them to work, but...

He closed his eyes.

He didn't want to watch.

He heard Parsons whisper.

"Good girl," he said. "Hold still now."

And the gun fired.

⁂

CHAPTER TWENTY FOUR
WE DID THIS TO OURSELVES

KAREN COULD FEEL her pulse beating behind her left eye, pinched closed by the angry red weal still growing above her brow. Her cheek felt warm, and at her feet she saw drips of blood spatter on the bare steel floor of the truck, but her arms were bound behind her back by plastic ties. She could only guess at the damage the rifle butt had dealt her by judging the pain.

It felt as if her head was about to explode.

"Mommy, my hands hurt," sniffed Emily, sandwiched between Ramos and a silent soldier sitting on the opposite side of the truck. Her own arms were tied behind her back, but the soldier just stared impassively no matter how angrily Karen yelled that she was just a child. For ten minutes he hadn't so much as blinked as Karen threw every curse word she knew at him, and eventually she'd given up trying.

"It won't be long now, pumpkin, I promise" she whispered hoarsely, attempting a smile that sent her forehead throbbing with renewed force. "As soon as we get where we're going they'll take those things off you."

Ramos leaned down to Emily, nuzzling the side of his head against hers, since there was no more comforting move he could make with bound hands. "It'll be OK, honey, don't worry." He turned to the soldier on the other side of the little girl, and his lip curled.

"You know we're US citizens? You have no right to hold us. We were on a public highway. You guys are going to jail for a long time for what you did to the boys in that car."

The soldier didn't even turn his head, and Ramos only fell silent when Valerie nudged him with her knee and sternly shook her head. *Don't antagonize him*, she said with her eyes.

For another ten minutes they rode on in tense silence, struggling to stay upright on the wooden bench seats that lined either side of the back of the truck as it bounced over rough terrain. Through the flap in the canvas covering at the back Karen could only see endless sun bleached wheat fields, broken by occasional high barbed wire fences as they seemed to slow through checkpoints.

Eventually the truck pulled to a stop, and as the hydraulic brakes hissed the soldier sitting beside Emily came alive as if he were powered by clockwork. He stood, holding his rifle at the ready as he brushed past their legs, and when he pushed aside the canvas and hopped down to the ground Ramos couldn't seem to resist raising his voice.

"You'd better just shoot us now, amigo, because when I get out of here I'm going to sue your ass to kingdom come!"

At that Valerie lost her patience. She raised her shoe and stamped hard on Ramos' foot, her face contorted with rage.

"What in all that's holy do you think you're doing, Cesar? You keep up like that and you're gonna get us all killed!" She pressed down on his foot again, harder this time. "Keep. Your mouth. *Shut.*"

Ramos tugged his foot out from beneath Valerie's, shaking the blood back into it with a wince. "What do you mean, killed? It's the damned Air Force, and we're American citizens. OK, they shot those guys in the car, but I'm guessing they refused to stop when they were ordered. We've just been arrested. We're not armed, and they know we're not a threat. The worst that'll happen to us is a slap on the wrist for wandering into the wrong field, right?"

Valerie lowered her voice to a harsh whisper. "Well sure, we'll get a slap on the wrist if they're the good guys, but what the hell makes you so sure who they are? It's not like you can identify them on sight."

Karen leaned forward, precariously balancing on the edge of her seat. "What do you mean, the good guys? They're the Air Force. What else would they be?"

Valerie blinked with surprise. For a long moment she just stared at Karen, her mouth hanging open, before she finally managed to speak.

"Oh my God," she muttered, her eyes wide. "You really don't know, do you?"

Karen shot a glance out through the gap in the canvas before leaning in and lowering her voice to a whisper. "Know what?"

Valerie shook her head in disbelief. "You don't know what's really going on here."

Karen's voice strained with frustration. "Val, we told you we haven't seen a TV since yesterday. We don't have a damned clue what's going on!"

Valerie opened her mouth to reply, but before she could speak the canvas was swept aside once more. Two soldiers climbed up to the back of the truck, and on the ground behind them a third pointed to Ramos.

"Him first," he said. The two men each took an arm and lifted Ramos to his feet, shoving him to the back of the truck and forcing him down to ground level, his hands still tightly bound behind his back. When his feet hit the ground he stumbled and fell face first, vanishing from Karen's view.

"Where are you taking him?" Karen demanded, trying to stand as the soldiers hopped down to the ground, She fell forward painfully onto the steel floor of the truck as they whipped down the canvas flap and pinned it in place, sealing them in darkness.

"Mommy!" Emily squealed as Karen hit the ground. "Are you OK?"

Karen winced at the sharp pain cutting into her wrists, and she rolled to her side and managed to take a breath. "I'm alright, pumpkin, it's OK." There was no way she could lift herself back into her seat, so she stayed where she was, her cheek pressed against the hot floor, breathing the layer of dust that covered the steel.

"Before they take me," she gasped, turning to face Valerie, "tell me what's going on."

Valerie leaned forward on the balls of her feet, lowering her voice to a whisper so it wouldn't carry beyond the truck.

"It was *us*," she said, her eyes wide with fear. "It wasn't terrorists who sent the missiles."

Karen stared up at the woman, certain she was delusional. She couldn't possibly believe something that insane. "What are you talking about?"

As the canvas flap swept back yet again and the soldiers climbed aboard to take another of them, Valerie stood and presented herself to them, allowing them to grab her arms. As they silently pushed her towards the back of the truck she turned and met Karen's eyes one last time.

"Karen, we did this to ourselves."

•▼•

CHAPTER TWENTY FIVE
ONE NEW MESSAGE

JACK DIDN'T WANT to open his eyes.

He didn't want to see Boomer's body. He wanted to remember her as she was, not laid out at the feet of the sheriff, his revolver still smoking. The memory of the gunshot repeated in his mind, and even if he didn't have the image in his head he knew the sound would haunt him forever.

But then another sound came, this one unexpected.

"What the f—"

That was the voice of Ray.

Jack opened his eyes to a scene that made no sense to him. Boomer was still at the sheriff's feet, alive but terrified, shivering and eyes wide in fright at the sound of the gunshot. Above her Parsons stood, but he looked down in confusion at his chest, staring at a growing bloom of red spreading out across his shirt. As Jack watched he took a staggering step back, then another, and then he stumbled to his knees.

A few steps behind him Ray held Jack's pistol out ahead of him, pointing it over Jack's shoulder at something behind him. He squeezed the trigger and Jack screamed at his legs to throw him out of the way, but the gun only gave a metallic click.

It was empty.

Jack had no clue what was going on, but finally his legs began to respond to his orders. With a burst of power he forced himself to his feet and barreled forward towards Ray. As the man dropped Jack's empty gun and fumbled at his holster for his own, Jack covered the distance between them in just a couple of seconds before he threw himself at Ray's waist, his full weight driving into his belly. The man doubled over with a pained grunt, folding to the floor. The gun went skittering out of his hands and across the asphalt.

Jack pulled himself up on his elbows, ready to rain blows on the man below him, but through the red mist he could see there was no need. Ray was out cold, knocked out when his head thunked against the asphalt.

He rolled off the unconscious man, still trying desperately to get his bearings. Beside the police cruiser the sheriff was slumped to the ground, his immense body still, a pool of blood spreading out around him. A few steps from him Cathy held herself in an alert crouch, confused and uncertain what was happening. Boomer lay flat on the ground, still frozen in fear but apparently unharmed.

And then Jack saw it. Standing by Cathy's truck, his tweed jacket bunched up as he held his arms out in front of him, Garside stood with Cathy's gun clutched tightly in his hands. He stared ahead at the body of the sheriff, the gun still trained on him.

"Doug," Jack said quietly, afraid that any sound might make him squeeze the trigger again. "Doug, are you OK?"

Garside's hands began to tremble. With a blink he seemed to come to, and he looked down at the gun almost as if he hadn't realized he was holding it.

"He... he shouldn't have threatened the dog," Garside muttered, slowly lowering the gun until his hand hung limp at his side. "He shouldn't..."

Now he carefully lowered the gun to the ground and took a step back from it, a look of shock on his face.

"Oh, God, what did I do?" His eyes were as wide as saucers as he stared at the sheriff's body. "Jack, I shot a policeman! I... I didn't mean... *What did I do?*"

Jack carefully approached Garside, kicking the gun away as he reached it, and he wrapped his arms around the Englishman's shivering shoulders.

"You saved us, Doug," he said, smiling. "It's OK. You saved our lives."

Garside pulled away in shock. "But... but I shot a policeman. Look," he pointed to the Parsons' prone body as Jack led him gently towards the police cruiser. "Look, I killed him. He's dead."

Jack turned to Cathy as he led Garside to the rear door of the cruiser. "Are you OK, Cathy? Are you hurt?"

Cathy shook her head, her face pale but her body intact. "No, I'm... I don't know how, but I think I'm alive."

"Then let's get the hell out of here before anyone else shows up." He pulled open the door of the car and carefully guided Garside onto the back seat.

"Are you taking me to prison?" Garside asked in a shaky voice, looking up at Jack with glazed eyes.

"No, Doug," Jack replied in a kindly voice. "I'm taking you to get a nice hot cup of tea, and then we're going to find your wife. Doesn't that sound good?"

Garside nodded, his face drained of color and his hands trembling. A wan smile flitted across his face.

"I think I'd quite like a cup of tea, yes. But then I think I'll have to go to prison. I shot a policeman, Jack."

Cathy appeared beside Jack, in one hand holding Boomer by the collar and in the other clutching the sheriff's revolver. Her own gun she'd picked up and tucked back into its holster at her waist. "It's OK, Doug," she said, pushing Boomer into the back of the cruiser before climbing in beside Garside. "He wasn't really a cop. He was just an asshole with a badge."

"But I killed him," Garside insisted, trembling as Cathy tugged off her jacket and draped it over Doug's shoulders.

"Good," she said, wrapping her arms around him and holding him close. "Jack, I think we should find that cup of tea sooner rather than later. I don't know how to treat shock, but I think tea might be a big part of it."

Garside stared at Jack as he climbed in the front seat and turned the key. "Yes, tea. I'd quite like a cup of tea."

Jack nodded and smiled in the rear view as he pulled the cruiser back out into the street, maneuvering around the sheriff's body and Ray, still unconscious on the asphalt. "You've earned that tea, buddy. Let's go find it."

As the cruiser passed Ray's pickup and the road stretched out ahead of them Jack suddenly felt a rush of optimism. He had no idea why. They'd lost half a day in Plumas Creek. He'd almost been imprisoned by a bunch of prepper lunatics, and he'd almost lost his dog and his new friends. The only win had been leaving in a car with... he glanced at the fuel gauge... with a full tank of gas, and it had almost ended in disaster.

But still Jack felt euphoric. As the sign for the turnoff to highway 89 approached he felt a sudden rush of energy. He felt as if he was beginning the final leg of the journey. He didn't know how, but he *knew* he was just a few short hours away from seeing his little girl again, somewhere out there in the abandoned vastness of California that spread out ahead of them.

Jack guided the cruiser around the corner as he passed the sign for the 89, and he smiled in the rear view as Boomer curled up in Garside's lap and settled in for a nap. The sun was high overhead, the road empty and—

A musical tone caught his ear, four notes that sounded familiar. He frowned, trying to place the tone, and when he finally realized what it was his heart skipped a beat.

He reached into his pocket, and when he drew it out he was holding his cell phone. The cracked screen lit up to a background of tropical sands, an old picture of Karen and the kids on vacation in Cancun.

He stared at the screen, transfixed by the vision. Somehow the phone had dried out in his pocket well enough to work again, and he felt his heart race a little faster as he realized he could once again read Karen's final message. He tapped the screen, keeping one eye on the road as he navigated to the inbox and looked for—

A notification popped up on the screen, and the shock at the sudden vibration of the phone was enough to send it tumbling out of his hand. It landed in the footwell beneath his feet, and in a panic he stepped on the brake and stopped in the middle of the road.

Bending at the waist he hunted for it with his fingers, nudging it until he could reach down and grab it, and when he pulled it back from beneath the seat and caught a look at the words glowing on the screen he felt his breath catch in his throat.

1 new message
Karen

He tapped the screen, and when the text appeared a smile spread across his face. He stepped on the gas and powered the cruiser forward.

Now he knew where he had to go.

He knew where to find his little girl.

●▼●

COMING SOON

NOTHING IS QUITE as it seems.

Jack now knows exactly where to find his ex-wife and little girl. Across the vast abandoned wasteland of California he's tracked them down. They're headed toward a place they've been promised will be safe.

Nowhere is safe.

Now Jack faces a race against time to rescue Karen and Emily before they discover the terrifying truth. Before they learn that they're walking into the lion's den.

Before they learn that Condition Black is even more horrifying than they could ever have imagined.

The concluding novel of the Jack Archer post-apocalyptic survival series will be released exclusively at Amazon, coming soon.

Printed in Great Britain
by Amazon